R. J. Park[er]'s creative career began [...] editor and producer. It was this back[...] series of cinematic, high-concept thrillers that grabs the reader from the very first page and doesn't release them until the last. R. J. Parker now lives in Salisbury.

richard-parker.com

twitter.com/Bookwalter
facebook.com/RJParkerUK
instagram.com/bemykiller

THE REMOVAL MAN

R. J. PARKER

One More Chapter

a division of HarperCollins*Publishers*

1 London Bridge Street

London SE1 9GF

www.harpercollins.co.uk

HarperCollins*Publishers*

1st Floor, Watermarque Building, Ringsend Road

Dublin 4, Ireland

This paperback edition 2022

First published in Great Britain in ebook format

by HarperCollins*Publishers* 2022

Copyright © R. J. Parker 2022

R. J. Parker asserts the moral right to

be identified as the author of this work

ISBN: 978-0-00-844798-4

Printed and bound in the UK using 100% Renewable Electricity

by CPI Group (UK) Ltd

To the dynamic Brewster family – Lee, Marielle, Joseph and Annabel – the sort of true friends you only meet a couple of times in your life.

Chapter One

Rose folded her arms across her chest and shivered in the cold air blasting through the open front door. She watched and flinched as the beloved green paisley couch that she liked to lounge on while she read was unceremoniously loaded into the back of the removal van by two paunchy and red-faced middle-aged men. Both of them seemed puffed out before they'd even started and she wondered if she'd actually end the evening calling them an ambulance. Maynard was monitoring them. It was his firm and they'd been pretty unreliable. They were the only local one, though, which was probably why they could afford to be so complacent. He had his hands on his thin waist, his thumbs jammed under the flap at the bottom of his brown corduroy jacket.

'OK, that's the lot.' Maynard let his two employees climb awkwardly down before rattling the door shut.

The two men caught their breath in the fading pink light. The one with ear and nose rings bent forward and rested his hands on his knees while the other secured the door.

Maynard strolled back up the drive, an insincere smile already primed for Rose. 'OK, we're full up for this trip. If you can just give me a signature.' He held out a digital screen, but he was still a few steps away.

'Sure.' She extended her hand but he slowed his pace, almost as if he wanted her to hold her arm out longer. Something about Maynard's impish manner made her uncomfortable. He was probably in his early sixties and had only the top row of his teeth bleached. The bottom ones were more noticeably yellow because of it. And she didn't like the way he'd ruffled her son's hair. Who honestly did that to other people's kids anymore?

'Use your finger.' He handed her the unit.

She signed the screen and released a breath of relief. After two no-shows, the heavy furniture she couldn't shift herself was finally headed for storage. 'So you'll pick up the boxes on Monday?' Rose noticed how echoey her voice was now that the hall had been emptied of cabinets.

'Absolutely. Should be about 8.30 but we'll call when we're on our way.'

'Remember to call my mobile. The landline has been disconnected.' She'd told him that already, but when they'd turned up at three instead of midday, Maynard had said

2

he'd tried to phone her on it. She suspected he hadn't. 'You've got that number now?'

'Yes,' he replied dismissively but his eyes were looking beyond her into the house.

Rose wondered if Maynard's silvery mop of hair was actually a wig. As she'd watched him rallying the other two, she'd noticed that the back of his neck was completely smooth. 'See you Monday then.' She looked at his hair closer but Maynard's eyes refocused on her.

'Just the two of you in the house then?'

That made her even more uncomfortable. 'My husband's home later.'

He nodded a little too emphatically. As if he suspected it was a lie. 'Have a good weekend then.' He gave her his lemon meringue smile again and trotted back down the drive.

The van bearing the legend 'Ty Maynard Dependable Removals' started up before he reached it and she watched him jump up into the cab before the vehicle surged away down the narrow country road, sending crows noisily bursting from a nearby tree.

Chapter Two

'Just for tonight.' Noah's fawn-brown eyes pleaded.

Rose could see his father in them. He used to employ the same tactic and got his way far too often. Her nine-year-old son had quickly adopted the strategy to get her committed to any short-term arrangement before she found herself unable to refuse the inevitable appeals to extend whatever it was she hadn't wanted to do in the first place. 'Once you get that tent set up, you'll want us to be in there all weekend.'

Noah looked affronted. 'Just tonight. Honest to God.'

Rose tried not to smirk. 'I've told you not to say that.'

She knew she was about to give in. Even though she was full of nduja pizza and had drunk two glasses of red wine. Even though it was April and the evenings were still cold.

'Isn't this like camping already though?' She gestured around the lounge.

Noah cast his eyes about the cardboard boxes stacked around them. 'No,' he stated categorically, shaking his head and pulling a comically long face for emphasis.

She was only playing for time. Rose wouldn't refuse him, but not because her discipline was lax. She was stricter with Noah than most of the others in her parents' group, but he hadn't complained the whole time they'd been in moving limbo. She and Noah had both said their goodbyes to the house weeks ago but the people buying had had issues with their sale. The agent had suggested putting it back on the market, but Rose had said they'd wait.

It was a kindness to say the house they'd lived in for seven years was a fixer-upper. Built in 1902, what the property lacked in solid foundations it made up for in runaway damp. Previously a guest house, the rooms had been converted but each of the doors still had a different key. They'd turned one into Lucas's pottery studio but that had been redundant long before the house went up for sale.

Everything else was now packed up and ready to go. Thirty-four boxes. Coincidentally, one for every year of her life. Was that all it amounted to? It had taken three months of viewings before she'd had a solitary, significantly lower offer from a foster couple who needed four bedrooms. But Rose really didn't want to let them down.

It was their third week of eating on a flat packing case. Noah had loved it to begin with and would have quite happily had junk food for breakfast, lunch and dinner. But with the couch gone, their everyday furniture and oven already in a storage facility near their new address and the pair of them now having to sleep on folding beds, the fun of living in a maze of taped-up boxes had seriously started to fray. Plus, Noah had just spent his Saturday helping her fill the last boxes, carrying them from the cellar and setting them in the hallway. How could she say no?

'I really don't want to sleep outside.'

'I'm not asking you to. I'll be fine on my own.'

'You said that before, but you only lasted half an hour.'

'I was only young then,' he countered, mortified.

Rose chuckled inwardly. That had been less than two years ago. She eyed the remaining slices of sourdough pizza in the box on top of the packing case. 'You haven't finished your dinner.'

Noah didn't respond. He knew it was a stalling tactic and waited for her gaze to return to his.

'It's going to get cold out there,' she warned.

'I'll wear a jumper over my pjs.'

'The tent's still got a hole in it.'

'It's not raining.'

'It's forecast though.'

'I won't sleep under the hole.'

'It'll be dark.'

'I've got my penlight.'

He'd been inseparable from the gadget since Lucas had bought it for him two Christmases ago. Rose sighed. If she let him sleep outside, she would end up out in the cold too. She picked up her glass of red and took a sip as if considering her answer, even though it was a foregone conclusion.

Noah replicated her sigh, rested his elbow on the low packing case and then put his face in his hand so his face wrinkled up. The left side of his light auburn hair jutted as it always did, like he'd just been sleeping on it. No matter what she did, it never seemed to flatten. She tied her identical but longer hair up into a ponytail and he regarded her expectantly.

Their Edwardian house with its rotting parquet floors was on its own at the edge of Hampton Forest. She'd always felt isolated there, but Lucas had enjoyed the seclusion for his work. He hadn't seemed quite as keen on its remoteness after the attempted break-in. That had rattled them both but they'd managed to keep it a secret from Noah. That was nearly three years ago but now that Lucas was absent, the episode had taken on a new implication for a mother alone with her child. She told herself it was a one-off event, that lightning was unlikely to strike twice, but it made her doubly vigilant when it came to security. She'd looked into getting an alarm system fitted but the cost for the old property was eye-watering. Their new place was on the third floor of a residential block. Only days to go now before they got in there. Was she being hyper cautious? The rear lawn was secure and surrounded by tall red-brick walls, but she still felt uncomfortable with the idea of her son out there in the dark. Their nearest neighbours were a drive away and beyond the tall back wall was nothing but dense forest. She'd fought with Lucas about letting Noah play there. Hampton Forest was private land used for deer and pheasant shoots so she'd used that as an excuse to keep her son away from it. Lucas said there was no harm out of season but, particularly after the attempted break-in, Rose felt nervous about who could be lurking in the trees. She and Lucas argued about leisure time for Noah. Rose didn't like tents and camping and preferred parks and hotels, but her husband loved their new bucolic lifestyle. Since Lucas hadn't been around, she hadn't done anything like that with Noah. She knew he missed it and felt guilty she couldn't do some of the outdoorsy things he wanted. Also, where they were moving didn't even have a balcony. Shouldn't they make the most of this before they had to leave?

'So…'

Rose swallowed the last of the wine in her glass and knew she was heading for a third. It had already relaxed her but she needed it today. Today was an anniversary. A date that only Rose observed. But now she'd have to sleep with one eye on the window.

'I'll move my bed there so I can keep watch.' She nodded to the double glazing they'd had installed that overlooked the lawn.

'I'll be OK on my own,' he said, aggrieved.

But it wasn't dark yet.

'So, I *can* pitch the tent?' There was that entreating look of his father's again. Its familiarity used to be an anchor for her but now his presence was a dead weight dragging her down to anxiety.

'Under the tree.' It was halfway up the lawn. He wouldn't be too far from the back door.

'OK.' He knew when to submit.

'Go and get it set up before I change my mind.'

Noah was quickly on his feet and rushed out of the back lounge to get the tent from the boxes in the hall.

Rose closed both their laptops, picked up a piece of cold pizza and then dropped it back on the greaseproof paper. As a dietician, she spent five days a week creating healthy eating plans for her patients at Petworth General. She wondered what they would make of her current habits. She emptied the tiny droplet in her glass and thought about the half-full bottle in the kitchen. One more.

Four hours later, she was sitting bolt upright on her folding bed, her heart in overdrive. It was pitch dark outside and somebody was banging hard on the window.

Chapter Three

At first, Rose briefly forgot she'd moved her folding bed downstairs and widened her eyes to let in as much information as possible. Something clattered to the floor. Her phone. That was it – she was in the back lounge, her blankets tangled around her feet.

The thumping on the window made her spin her head to the floor-to-ceiling double-glazed windows. Beyond the glass was pitch black and rivulets of water were cascading down the pane. It was raining hard. Rose squinted at the darkness but could see only the reflection of the paper shade lamp she'd positioned in front of it to reassure Noah. She'd left the upstairs lights on too.

She waited for his face at the pane, felt her heart's rapid pump in her throat.

'Noah?' She threw the blanket aside and put her bare feet on the cold floor. She'd been hot as she'd fallen asleep but now chill air wafted into the scoop neck of her white nightshirt. She briefly registered her phone on the floor but stood shakily and squinted at the window. 'Noah?' Her right leg trembled and she felt a little dizzy.

Only the sound of trickling rain replied, and she quickly wiped at her eyes. What time was it? She'd told herself she'd stay awake. How long had she been asleep? Noah had set the tent up before eight and she'd been surprised at how eager he was to be left alone. After she'd made sure he was warm, had his inhaler and was tucked up in his sleeping bag, she'd kissed the top of his head. He'd been reading a graphic novel by his penlight and had said goodnight without looking up.

The door rattled and Rose leapt back a pace. 'Noah?' The handle was being tried but she'd told him she'd left the back door open if he needed to get in to use the toilet. That gave him the option to come back inside to sleep too.

Rose bent down and swiftly slid the lamp on the floor away from the window, so it no longer illuminated the glass. But she couldn't make out any shapes in the blackness beyond the double glazing.

'Noah.' She didn't like the uncertainty in her voice.

A board creaked under her weight as she readjusted her footing. A strong driving gust of wind opened up a circle in the vertical droplets on the window. How long had it been raining? She couldn't allow Noah to stay out there in that leaky tent.

A hand appeared at the handle and it rattled again.

Rose stayed where she was, her body rigid.

It was a small hand, the fist under the outside handle as the frame shook. Noah's face appeared as he tried to shove it open.

Rose exhaled, went to the door and lifted up the catch. It slid unsteadily open on the runner and her son squeezed through the gap as soon as it was wide enough. His hair was flattened by the rain.

'I've been banging for ages.'

That was one of his exaggerations, but Rose felt an immediate pang of guilt at having fallen asleep and not letting him in straightaway. 'Why didn't you use the back door?' She felt his soaked hair and then the shoulders of the navy dressing gown he had on over his pyjamas and jumper.

'I tried to. I couldn't get in.' He looked down at his soaked red slippers.

Rose took her blanket from her bed and wrapped it around him. 'Are you sure?'

Noah nodded emphatically from the end of the blanket tunnel. 'The handle turned but the door wouldn't open. Honest to God.'

'Don't say that.' She rubbed his hair vigorously and then lowered the blanket to his shoulders. 'Let's take a look.'

Rose led him down the passage of boxes to the kitchen doorway. Noah had said they were like trenches in pictures he'd seen of the First World War and now she couldn't shake the image.

She turned on the light and entered the kitchen where her collection of potted succulents was lined up on the draining board, ready for relocation. She stopped in her tracks a foot away from the back door.

Noah shuffled in behind her. 'I don't know why it wouldn't open.'

But Rose immediately did. The bolt was over at the top. Had she done that without thinking? She was tired and she'd had another glass of wine. Only three glasses. Big glasses though. She'd put the rest of it in the cupboard because she'd wanted to keep a watchful eye on Noah. Had she locked up on autopilot? She had no recollection of it.

'You locked it.' Noah walked past her and pointed upwards.

Rose reacted as if she hadn't already noticed. 'That's... I don't remember that.'

Noah regarded her with deep mystification.

There was no mitigating this. 'I'm sorry... I must have done it without thinking.'

'Did you have more of that drink?' Noah looked about the kitchen as if he'd see evidence of it.

As he often did, Noah had become a mini-Lucas.

'No. You saw how much I had.' *Except the one she'd had after settling him in the tent.* Here she was, again justifying herself to her nine-year-old son. But she couldn't remember bolting the door and now she felt terrible that she'd shut him out there. What if he hadn't been able to wake her?

Noah shivered and wrapped the blanket tighter around himself.

She went to him and kneeled. 'I *am* sorry.' But she suspected he might be milking the performance. He knew full well what treats 'sorry' from his mother often meant. 'Why did you come in? Did you need to pee?'

Noah shook his head. 'No. I think someone's out there.'

R ose tried not to allow the tiny spike of alarm she felt register on her face and resisted the temptation to immediately turn back in the direction of the lounge. She'd left the double-glazed door open.

'Why would you think that?'

'I heard them,' he stated simply.

It had happened before. The last time Noah and Lucas had camped on the lawn, an animal had been circling the tent because they'd been cooking food on a mini barbecue, but Noah couldn't be placated. They'd come in before midnight and her son hadn't wanted to repeat the experience until Lucas had taken him on a kayaking trip to Hampton Lake that summer.

'Could it have been one of our foxes?' Rose was a city girl and still hadn't got used to the unnerving, childlike braying the creatures made at night.

17

'No,' he replied after brief consideration.

'What did you hear?'

'Noises, like someone was pulling something.'

'Pulling something?'

'Dragging something heavy along. Every time I shone my torch out of the tent, there was nobody there.'

'There you go then.' But Rose didn't believe her own assurance. 'Maybe it was from the other side of the wall. Something in the forest.'

'No. It sounded much closer than that.'

Rose shivered inwardly. 'Things sound stranger at night. When you can't see anything.'

Noah didn't look convinced.

She lowered the towel from his head and brushed his wet hair from his eyebrows. 'Would you feel better if we took a good look outside?'

He hated her playing with his hair now, but he didn't pull away. He was clearly spooked.

He nodded.

It was the last thing she wanted to do. 'OK. Let me just get some slippers—'

A sliding sound from the lounge.

They both tensed and Rose turned back in the direction of the noise.

Nothing more. Just the light patter of rain on the skylight.

Rose stood straight, her attention directed down the trench of boxes beyond the doorway.

'What was that?' Noah asked without opening his mouth. Rose kept her gaze on the dingy lounge. The cold of the floor tiles travelled up through her bare feet to her shoulders.

'Ssshhh, listen,' she whispered.

Noah whispered as well. 'What can you hear?'

'Wait.' *You're scaring each other now*, she told herself. She didn't blink, just kept her eyes locked ahead.

Noah's hand grabbed the back of her nightshirt.

Rose reached behind her, put a comforting hand on his arm. She felt her shirt go tight across her as he tightened his grip.

'Stay here,' he begged.

She could hear the terror in his voice. Rose eyed the paring knife on the little chopping board. The knife block had been packed away. How terrified would Noah be if she picked that up? She hoped she was overreacting – it was just Noah's story about there being someone outside that was unsettling her.

But Rose briefly cast her mind back to the attempted break-in they'd had in 2019 and how she'd told Lucas he was overreacting when he'd gone downstairs to investigate a noise. He said he saw someone looking in through the hallway window, but they'd run off before he'd got the front door open. She'd been unsettled for months after.

Another low hiss from the lounge.

Rose tried to swallow quietly but couldn't conceal the sound from Noah. She wanted to shout a warning but knew that would alarm her son even more. If anyone came running at them, she could shut the kitchen door.

There was no lock on it. They could easily force their way through. There was no phone in here. And hers was on the floor of the room where the noise was coming from. She had no choice. Rose leaned forward and picked up the paring knife.

Chapter Five

'C lose the door,' Noah said, vocalising her thoughts.

But Rose remained frozen, staring unblinkingly at the area beyond the walls of boxes. An icy draught tightened the goosebumps on the backs of her arms. The wind was blowing into the house through the open double-glazed door.

They both waited. Rose counted the minutes in her head. Three passed without another sound from the lounge.

'I really need to pee now,' Noah hissed.

So did Rose. She clasped the little knife to her chest and counted another minute. Did that really mean there was nobody there or were they just standing motionless, waiting for her to make a move?

'I have to go.' He tugged at her nightshirt.

She held up a hand without turning. Rose realised the

rain had stopped. The house was silent now except for the almost indiscernible tick of the heating.

A sharp gust of wind and suddenly the main light came on in the lounge.

Rose reversed three paces, her hand grabbing the door handle in readiness to slam it.

But it was halfway closed when she froze.

'Shut it!' Noah yelled.

Rose shook her head. 'It's OK.'

'Quickly!'

'Look, it's fine.' She opened the door again so he could see.

The paper shade lamp she'd positioned on the floor had slid into view on its side. That was the sound they'd heard. It had been blown across the room by the wind through the door and now it had gusted further, so it illuminated the corridor of boxes.

Noah said nothing as he peered around her.

Rose wasn't one hundred per cent convinced either. But if he hadn't said he'd heard noises…

She kept the knife tight to her chest and took a step forward.

'Wait a bit longer.' Noah tugged her back.

'It's OK. I'll be two seconds.'

Noah tried to yank her back again.

'Let go.' Without taking her eyes off the lounge, she gently prised away his hand.

'If it's OK, why have you got a knife?'

'Ssshhh.' It was the noise she made when she didn't have an answer. She took another pace forward. 'Quiet.'

'Why should I keep quiet if there's nobody else here?'

Rose swallowed drily again and padded along the lounge floor until she reached the end of the box run. She paused there, then took a slow breath in. The lamp was at her feet. There was no other sound except the bay tree leaves hissing outside.

You're panicking. There's nobody else here. You're frightening Noah. Quickly look before he has an asthma attack.

Rose gripped the knife handle tightly and stepped into the room.

Nobody there. *Of course not.*

But she quickly flicked on the lights and double-checked every corner before turning back to Noah.

He was halfway up the passage of boxes, frozen midstep.

'All clear,' she said as if she'd known it all along and had just been indulging him. Rose felt a bubble of tension burst in her stomach and relief flood through her.

But when Noah joined Rose, they both stood silently for a moment as they looked at the ajar door and the dark gap to outside.

Chapter Six

'Will you look outside too?' Noah implored.

Rose moved over to the window and paused with her fingers on the handle. 'There's nobody there, but if you really want me to...' She wanted to close the gap and seal the door.

Noah stared past her through the black pane.

Rose reminded herself how unlikely it was that anyone could have climbed over the tall walls. She was creeping herself out. *It was only the wind blowing over the lamp.*

'Just to make sure.' He still didn't shift his eyes from the glass.

Rose sighed and shook her head. She really didn't want to go out there. It was cold and dark, and she just wanted to crawl back under her blankets. This was something Lucas would have done. But now it was her job. She saw the trepidation on Noah's face. Rose had to step up.

'Just a moment…' She pulled on her purple towelling nightrobe, pocketed the knife and slid her feet into her faux animal skin slippers.

'I'll come too.' Noah approached the window and squinted through his reflection.

Rose tensed and put her hand on the edge of the door.

'I've got my penlight.' Noah slid it out of his top pyjama pocket and offered it to her.

She took it from him. 'OK, this won't take long,' she said breezily, more to persuade herself than anything else.

'I want it back.'

She nodded absently and slid the door open further. A strong breeze blew against her, and she pulled her collar tighter around her neck before switching on the light.

Noah joined her on the paved area in front of the window but stood behind her.

Rose quickly darted the beam around, part of her dreading the spotlight illuminating something she didn't want to see. It lit up the back of Noah's orange one-man tent that was pitched under the tall bay tree and she played the yellow circle about it before skimming it along the grass and the tall walls either side of it.

'See? Nothing to worry about.' She tried not to let the relief register in her voice.

Noah was silent but stepped around to her right.

Rose felt braver and slowly zig-zagged the beam, starting at the far end of the lawn and working it back to where they were standing to cover every inch before them.

The wind picked up and the bay tree hissed.

Rose looked down at Noah and he was nodding slowly. The action speeded up as he conceded that there was nobody there.

'Come on, it's getting cold out here.'

'Can you tuck me in again?' Noah took a few paces towards the tent.

'You still want to sleep down there?' she asked incredulously.

Noah turned, frowning. 'Like you said, there's nothing to worry about.'

She marvelled at his about-face. She had allayed his fears, even though she still felt on edge.

Noah put out his hand. 'Can I have my penlight back?'

'Why don't you sleep inside now? The weather's better tomorrow.'

'I want to sleep out here tonight,' he wailed and bent over double like he always did when he knew she was going to refuse him.

A day meant nothing to her, but to a nine-year-old, it was like being made to wait a week. 'I could make some hot chocolate. And at least the wi-fi works indoors. I think you were brave to stay out here this long.' *Make it easy for him.*

Noah faltered, seemed tempted.

'I'm going in.' As she half-turned, she felt a stab of guilt. It was the easier option for her. Shouldn't she be spending time with Noah – time Lucas would have killed for?

'You go back to bed. I'm going to stick it out.'

She grimaced. That was the sort of pathos Lucas would have employed. 'You don't need to "stick it out".' Did she really want to deprive him of this or was she still shaken by what had just happened?

'I know that, but I want to,' he decided resolutely and turned back to the tent.

'Wait.' She held in another sigh. 'I'll come and say good night again.'

Noah swivelled back.

Rose could see the obvious relief on his face. Or did he realise he was about to get her to stay?

'You're sure you're going to be OK on your own?' She knew how this was about to play out. *Forget your comfy camp bed for tonight.* She pulled the door closed and followed him down towards the tent, her beam playing over its orange triangular rear.

As he reached it, she still felt uneasy. It was the only thing left that could still be a hiding place.

Chapter Seven

Your phone's still on the floor in the lounge, Rose told herself. She turned back to the door.

'I really need to pee now,' Noah announced and strode off down the lawn.

'Wait!' Rose called after him. 'Use the bathroom!'

'No time.' There was desperation in his voice.

Rose followed him with the beam and then aimed it at the tent. *Everything's OK. You're being ridiculous.* Soon she could hear the sound of trickling and her son's relief.

'Don't look,' he said with mortification as she briefly swung the light to him.

'OK, just… hurry it up.'

'I can't hurry.'

She shone the penlight at the tent and it fluttered in the wind. Rose trembled in the cold blast.

'OK, done.' Noah returned to her and took the light from her hand.

'Wait.' She followed him down the lawn.

He strode to the tent and as he ducked down and entered it, the light suddenly went out and Rose was in darkness.

'Noah.' She tried to keep the alarm from her voice. She had only been about eight feet from the tent, but she suddenly felt as if she were walking off course. She put her hands out and kept going, expecting the tent to light up at any moment. She slowed when it didn't. 'I can't…' She had to be almost on top of it. She waved her hands in front of her and anticipated her fingers brushing against its wet material.

A squeaking rustle from in front of her. Like Noah was sliding over his sleeping bag.

'Put your light back on. I can't see.'

The tent suddenly lit up to her right. She'd wandered past it and towards the unkempt border. She circled around to the front, which was about three feet away from the base of the bay tree. The door flaps were slightly parted, and she could see the muddy black soles of Noah's red slippers inside. It looked like he was kneeling down.

She knelt to the low entrance. 'I'll come in just for a minute.' Rose told herself everything was fine. She'd tuck him in and see how he felt. If it looked like they were both going to stay out there, she'd dash back to the house and get her phone. Lucas had slept in here with Noah before and he was nearly six foot. Rose was only five three. She stood again and looked back up the lawn towards the illuminated lounge. Even with its stacks of boxes, it looked a hundred times more inviting than the tent.

A low murmuring from inside.

What was that? A male voice? She grunted as she bent to her knees again and listened.

'Noah?' Parting the flaps, she slipped inside. The interior smelt mouldy.

Noah was on his knees.

'What's that?'

His body shifted slightly but his beam was pointing away so there was little light to work out what he was doing.

The murmuring got louder.

'Shine your light back here. I can't see.'

It was suddenly in her face, and she squinted against it.

A harsh buzz as Noah shuffled in front of her.

Rose put her hand to her eyes. 'What are you doing?'

Voices emerged from the static again. It was a radio.

The light dropped to the floor and Rose could make out Noah as he turned and sat at the end of the tent and shone the beam onto Lucas's digital radio.

'I thought we'd packed that away.' Rose moved inside the tent and crawled forward on her stomach so her face was by Noah's knees.

Noah shone the torch under his chin so his features looked scary.

'It's too late to be listening to that now. You should have been asleep hours ago.' But she still didn't know what time it was. It felt late.

Noah didn't answer, just kept the torch under his chin.

Rose could hear his breathing.

'Noah Dunbar, don't do that or I'm going straight back in.'

Noah held the position for a little while longer and then directed the light at the radio. 'If I leave it on, we won't be able to hear any noises outside.'

'Is that sensible? If someone is out there, we don't want them to catch us unawares.'

Noah considered that for a moment and then switched off the two chatting voices.

What was she doing? She didn't want to scare him all over again. His reaction had given her a small dose of satisfaction though. Lucas used to do a thing she hated when they went to bed. He'd turn off the light but not get under the duvet. He'd just stand there by the light switch breathing and not answering her. It freaked her out and, at some point, Noah had started doing it to her too.

'Not that there is anybody out there, though,' she added dismissively. 'I think we've established that beyond doubt.'

Noah rested the penlight on top of the radio so it illuminated them both. 'I definitely heard something.'

'I'm not saying you didn't. It was probably in the forest though. Sound plays tricks at night. Take your slippers off and get back in your sleeping bag.'

Noah obeyed and a few moments later, he was snuggled up with the edge of his indigo sleeping bag under his chin.

'You look like a blue snake.'

He smiled broadly and Rose draped a blanket over both of them.

'You don't have a pillow.' His face wrinkled in concern.

'That's OK.' She rested her head on her palm. She couldn't possibly sleep here.

Noah closed his eyes.

It never took him long to fall asleep once he'd run out of negotiating power or was, as now, overcome by exhaustion.

She watched him for a while but didn't move. She'd give it a few minutes and then she'd turn off the light. Then another few before she slid herself out of the tent. She was pretty comfortable now. They hadn't slept in the same bed since he was five. Maybe she should make the most of it as long as her back allowed her. Those three glasses of wine were certainly helping...

Rose listened as his breathing got louder and shallower, then turned off the penlight and decided to close her eyes for just a few moments.

A low whimper.

Rose opened them, the smell of cut grass and earth suddenly pungent. She blinked at the darkness and it felt like there were small pieces of gravel under her eyelids. Hay fever misery. That's why she hated camping trips. She was ten again, waking in the night and not knowing if she was alone or not.

A short intake of breath from nearby.

Rose sat upright. So her mother had come back. She'd told her that she would be back for dinner, but Rose had heated some beans and sausages in a saucepan over the gas stove and eaten on her own before putting herself to bed. There had been a few other families staying on the muddy site but they all had young children. Nobody her age. It hadn't bothered her. She had her library books with her and she'd passed the evening in her sleeping bag with a yellowing Daphne du Maurier. She'd gone to sleep at about nine when there had still been no sign of her mother. She'd said she was heading into the nearby village for an hour, but Rose knew what that meant. She would come back smelling of wine and wearing that sickly grin she always had to conceal her irresponsible parenting.

Since Rose's father had died, family life had fallen apart quickly and this last-minute trip had been no exception. Things had got thrown into the back of the car on Friday and it was away to the countryside – a place where Rose's antihistamines fought a losing battle. Rose didn't want a holiday. Didn't feel they should have one so soon after the funeral. She was happy to stay at home, but her mother seemed to believe that sleeping in claustrophobic nylon wasp catchers was somehow compensation for her previous bad behaviour.

She kept the canary yellow sleeping bag gathered at her chin but slid out of the zip door and stood up in it, shuffling towards her mother's tent that was pitched beside hers.

It sounded like her mother was crying again. She'd caught her in the past when she didn't think Rose was listening. But when she drank, there was no attempt to conceal it. It was distressing to see her like that – so vulnerable and oblivious to how it affected Rose. But now she'd seen it so many times she just went through the motions. Probably because she realised that the tears weren't for her father. It was self-pity. Her mother still hadn't accepted how much their life had changed. Rose had no choice but to become the grown-up.

The sound stopped.

So did Rose. Her feet halted their shuffle in the sleeping bag.

'Rose?'

She didn't answer. She knew her mother didn't want her daughter to see her like this.

Rose turned back in the direction of her own tent.

'That you?'

She started to pad back.

'It's OK. She's asleep.'

Rose halted and turned. Who was she talking to?

A murmur in response. A man.

Rose edged back.

'She won't hear.' The man's reassurance.

It was a smudgy voice. Just like her mother's after she'd been drinking the sloe gin she made at home.

Rose couldn't stop herself. Her father hadn't been dead five months.

As she parted the doors, she could see the impostor sprawled naked over her mother. Her mother's eyes opened. She saw Rose standing there, her dull regard on her for what felt like minutes while the stranger heaved away. Then she just closed them again, as if Rose's presence couldn't have been of smaller consequence.

Rose opened her eyes into darkness and the hay fever grit had evaporated. She released a breath, heard Noah's soft exhalations follow it. She wondered how long she'd fallen asleep with her son. A few minutes? A couple of hours? Clearly being in the tent with the smell of the lawn and earth in her nostrils had prompted the unwanted memory.

Noah continued to snore.

Could she slip out unnoticed and return to the house to get her phone and another pillow?

A long slow dragging noise interrupted the thought. It sounded like it was right outside the tent.

Chapter Eight

R ose raised her head from her palm and listened.
Nothing.

She tugged at the blanket so her ear was exposed to the cold air and held her breath. After remaining motionless for a full minute, she couldn't pick up the noise again. Her gaze flicked to Noah. His breathing had stopped. In the dingy light, she focused on his dark sockets and heard his eyelashes brush against his pillow as he blinked. He was awake.

'You heard it too?'

'Ssshhh.' Rose strained for the sound. It couldn't have been her circulation, the pressure of her ear on her hand. It was too loud.

'I told you.'

Rose pushed herself into a sitting position. It had sounded close. Very close. But the lawn had definitely been empty when they'd entered the tent. She fumbled for the penlight, and it clattered off the top of the radio.

'What are you going to do?' Noah whispered.

'I'm going to take a look.' Her circulation pumped fast in her temple as she cast the blanket aside, clicked on the penlight and crawled to the slit of the door. She wanted to zip it up tight. Instead, she paused there and waited.

'What can you see?' Noah didn't move.

The circle of light was on the open flaps of the tent. She parted them with her fingers and extended her arm, so the trunk of the bay tree was lit up. Rose waved the light from side to side again but there was nothing amongst the rose bushes at the base of the rear wall. Was there an animal skulking nearby? She could just hear the low hiss of the traffic on the main road and that other unidentifiable rumble of night. Wind? Aeroplanes? When it was dark, the neighbourhood had a different sound all its own.

A dog barked aggressively far off but fell silent. That was from the kennels. They were over three miles away but on a windless evening you could hear them like they were next door.

She had to leave the tent. *Just stand and shine the torch back towards the house. There's nothing there.*

'I'll go with you.'

She could feel the cold air clasp her face. 'No. Stay cosied up. I'll just be a second.' Rose remembered the knife in her pocket. She didn't want to take it out in front of Noah again, but it was good to know it was there. She tensed the muscles in her stomach and took her weight on her knees as she stood up and went out. Turning her body, she quickly pinged the beam of the torch around the lawn.

Nothing. No eyes of an animal caught in the light. No sign of anything.

The house looked so inviting. But she was here now. Hopefully that meant she wouldn't be expected to camp out tomorrow. See it through for Noah. Maybe he'd want to go back into the warmth as much as she did now though.

'Anything?' His voice tremored.

'All clear.' She turned and slid herself backwards into the tent again.

'You definitely heard it though?'

'Yes. I did.' Rose didn't lie down again but pulled the blanket around her where she sat cross-legged next to Noah. She positioned the penlight back on top of the radio.

'See. I wasn't making it up,' he said, no longer whispering.

'I didn't say you were. Perhaps it was something burrowing under the ground. A rabbit or a mole.' But she understood why it had frightened Noah. It had sounded so close.

They both sat in silence for a couple of minutes, seeing if it came again.

No dragging sound.

'I don't think I'm going to sleep now,' Noah eventually declared.

'Just close your eyes. You were snoring a minute ago.'

Rose knew how grouchy Noah got if his sleep was interrupted.

'I'll stay awake with you.'

'Don't worry about me. I've already had some shut eye. Do you want to go in?'

He shook his head once.

As pigheaded as his Dad. 'Should I switch off the light?'

'No,' he said sharply. 'Leave it on.'

'OK.' She was glad he wanted that. *This is crazy. You're meant to be the adult.* 'Let's talk for a bit then.'

Noah nodded.

It was clear he was prepared to do anything other than go to sleep and Rose was happy to take advantage. They used to have such good chats but lately Noah had got increasingly attached to his laptop and, even though she rationed his use of it, he spent much of the time he wasn't on it talking about how his friends were allowed more screen time than he was. 'What shall we talk about?'

'Dad.'

'OK,' she agreed uncertainly. He hadn't asked the inevitable since Wednesday. It was never an easy conversation for either of them. 'What about Dad?'

'Why doesn't he want to see me?'

Chapter Nine

'You know that's not true.' But that was becoming increasingly difficult to justify.

'It's been nearly three weeks.'

It had been and Rose knew he counted the days. 'He knows how busy you are with school,' she improvised feebly.

Noah fixed her with a cynical expression way beyond his years, eyelids drooped.

'I'll speak to him tomorrow though.' Rose said it like the situation could change but she'd said that so many times before.

He sighed at her familiar stalling tactic.

'How about some hot chocolate?'

Noah's face brightened but suspicion lingered. He knew she was misdirecting him. 'OK.'

'I *will* speak to him tomorrow.' She felt like she was deceiving him.

'With marshmallows?' He was letting her off the hook.

'Have you ever known me to make it any other way?' She started to crawl back to the door of the tent.

'You can tell me if he doesn't want to see me.'

His pained expression was too much to bear. She crawled back to him. 'Of course he does. Never think that. All right?'

He nodded but didn't seem convinced.

'Look at me,' she said sternly. 'There's nobody he'd rather see.'

'Honest to God?'

She was about to rebuke him but stopped herself. 'Remember when you broke your leg and Hazeem wanted to visit you here?'

'I know what you're going to say.'

'You didn't want Hazeem to see you with your leg in plaster.'

'That was different.'

It was. Hazeem was permanently in a wheelchair and her son had said he felt embarrassed for his friend to see him in one because Noah would only need it for a couple of months. 'It is kind of the same. Can you understand that your dad always wants to be strong for you? Like he's always been.'

'Yes,' Noah said flatly.

'He just wants to get better first.'

'But he may never get better.'

That was the first time Noah had ever said that. Even though it was true, it was something she thought she'd protected him from. She felt her throat tighten but fought it back. 'We never give up hope. And your father wants to get strong for you.' She kept her voice steady. 'That's why he thinks about you every day. You're his reason for getting better.'

Noah looked down at his sleeping bag and nodded again.

'So you have to be strong for him too.'

He didn't look up.

'I will speak to him, I promise. You'll see him soon, but you'll just have to be patient. We all have to be patient, like Doctor Woodhouse said.'

She knew why he was talking about his father. It would have been the two of them out here tonight. Lucas would make it a proper adventure. Noah loved her but she was no replacement for the male bonding that would normally be going on.

'And where's Grandma?'

Indeed. Where *was* Grandma? After Rose's father had died of leukaemia when she was ten, her mother had gone permanently off the rails. There'd been a lot of guilt because she'd been unfaithful to Rose's father during his illness and from then on, she'd pulled a series of disappearing acts throughout Rose's life, particularly when things got tough. True to form, she'd vanished with her new boyfriend soon after Lucas had gone into hospital. It was the one occasion Rose could really have used her support, but she'd long ago resigned herself to her mother's capriciousness.

'She'll be in touch... when she's ready.' Or when she needed money. The last time she'd said she'd needed the deposit for a house, but it had turned out to be a fund for her boyfriend's rehab.

'She promised to take me camping.'

'She's promised a lot of things.' They would have to leave it there. She wouldn't allow her to spoil their weekend. 'OK, you coming to get this hot chocolate with me?' She knew what his answer would be.

Noah pulled his sleeping bag tighter around him to demonstrate how comfortable he was.

'I thought so, you lazy rat. Give me five. If you're still awake when I get back—'

'I will be.'

She didn't doubt it. 'If you're still awake, I'll tell you the story about the couple lost in the woods...' She had no idea what that would be.

He narrowed his eyes at her. 'Couple lost in the woods?'

It sounded pretty vague to her, but she had the time it took the milk to boil to come up with something. 'Perhaps I shouldn't tell you in the dark.' She knew that was a red rag. Lucas had scared Noah with an urban legend about a murderer with a hook hand on their first lake camping trip and he'd been terrified, even when Lucas insisted it had all been make-believe. Now Noah lapped them up to prove he wasn't afraid. But she knew he still was.

'Back soon. Stay warm.' Were creepy stories really wise? It had certainly distracted him from an uncomfortable conversation, but she wasn't giving herself any points for that.

Rose pulled herself out of the tent and stood. She couldn't deny that she was still feeling uneasy. Perhaps it was the two awakenings she'd had. And now she had to cobble a story together to tell Noah. Not too frightening and nothing to do with ghosts. Noah was terrified by that idea. What could her story be about?

She headed back to the house and shivered against the icy air. Her breath clouded ahead of her but there was no chance of luring Noah back indoors. She'd get her phone and a spare jumper and lock the double glazing. The back door was still bolted. Maybe a story about a couple finding treasure in the woods. Cursed treasure. Keep it tame.

A crow rustily squawked in a treetop.

Rose reached the double-glazed doors but stopped as a movement in her peripheral vision caused her to look up at Noah's bedroom window.

The light wasn't on in there, but it was dimly lit by the bulb on the landing.

Somebody had been standing at the pane and had quickly shifted away. She'd seen their dark silhouette and the pale flash of their face.

Chapter Ten

R ose's limbs locked and her gaze remained fixed on
the semi-lit square of glass. But even though her
mind grappled for explanations, there was no doubting
what she'd just seen. It had definitely been a man's face.

She instinctively turned back to the tent and then
whipped back to the window as if the face might have
returned. No sign, but it *had* been there. Whoever it was
must have seen her walking up to the house. As Rose
exhaled fear in short irregular breaths, she wondered how
he'd got inside. Had he broken in through the front? Lucas
had had a double lock fitted after their last scare. She'd left
the double-glazed window open. Had he entered there?
Surely she would have heard it slide open from the tent.
And he would have to have scaled one of the back walls
first. Maybe he'd been circling the property and that's what

Noah had heard earlier. Her mouth opened but she stopped herself from yelling. There was nobody nearby to hear. The intruder had to have seen her, so the only person it would alarm would be Noah.

Rose's eyes remained wide and unblinking, her attention dead on the window as her hand went to her pocket. Shit. The knife wasn't there. It had probably dropped out in the tent when she'd lain down. Was she capable of using it anyway? Peering in through the closed double-glazed window, she could see her phone lying on the wooden floor. Should she quickly dash in and grab it? She tilted her eyes back up to the window again. Nobody there. She waited, listening for sounds from inside. If he knew she'd seen him, perhaps he'd flee. But the house was silent. Her heart beat tightly, like it was being squeezed by a fist.

She had to call the police. If the intruder was still upstairs, she could get in, grab the phone and race outside again. Call them from there. But what if he heard her? What if he came downstairs and pursued her onto the lawn? She swung her head briefly to the tent again. Noah was oblivious inside. She couldn't panic him. Had to get him out of danger as quickly as possible.

She fixed her eyes on Noah's bedroom window again and then scanned the others. No sign of movement. She took a pace towards the door. The phone was lying not six feet away from her, but she knew the door rattled when it opened. Would she be endangering Noah if she tried it? Her eyes darted to the boundary walls on either side of her. They were over nine feet tall. Would it be better for them both to try and escape over them and run to the nearest village to use a phone?

A clatter.

Rose jolted back a step. That had definitely come from inside. She held her breath, felt her whole frame throbbing.

She started to count but as she got past twenty, there had been no other sound. Had he left? If he had intended to rob her, the fact that most of their possessions were boxed and sealed might have put him off. Or he'd taken a look through the front window, seen everything packed up and the lack of furniture and thought the house was empty. Perhaps he believed he could take his time going through everything but had been surprised to see her walking up from a tent on the lawn. Chances were, he was already halfway down the road. But the lights had been on. Surely he'd have known someone was around. Maybe he knew he had a window of opportunity before the police could make the journey to her isolated address from town.

She couldn't go around the front to check without scaling the wall and she wasn't even sure she could get over it. Her only option was to open the double-glazed door. She took a pace towards it, ears alert for any other movement. She wouldn't go any further than the lounge. Just grab the phone and leave again. Call the police and wait outside with Noah until a car arrived.

Rose took the last three steps to the door and squinted at

the darkened doorway to the hall beyond the stacks of boxes. The front door was obviously still shut. Maybe he'd left through one of the windows of the other rooms. But a trickle of cold dread flowed faster inside her as she put her fingers on the cold metal of the handle. He's *still in there.*

She released it again. Stood back. *Let him finish. Take what he wants. Why risk going inside?*

A harsh wind shoved her back, but her body was too tense to shiver against it. *But he's seen you. He knows you're out here. Perhaps he's on his way down now.* The phone was her best chance.

Her hand went back to the handle and her wrist tautened. The metal gave under the pressure, and she cringed as it clicked, and the lock slid out of the frame. Her eyes were fixed on the darkened doorway to the hallway. Was he watching her from somewhere back there, waiting for her to step inside so he could close the door and deal with her without Noah hearing?

Rose flinched as she rattled the door slowly open half a foot but hovered outside. The smell of her home was on her face, warm and familiar, but she didn't blink as she put one slippered foot lightly on the floor. If there was any movement in front of her, she could quickly retreat and pull the door closed again. Could she hold it closed though? What would she do if they followed her outside? Noah couldn't scale the walls and she was positive she couldn't.

The phone was directly in front of her. She calculated

she probably only had to take three paces inside to grab it. But she didn't move and remained where she was as her breathing sounded suddenly loud in her head.

Chapter Eleven

Rose flitted her eyes between the darkened doorway and the phone on the floor as she painstakingly took a second step forward. Should she just lunge for it, quickly reverse and slide the door shut after her? Another pace would mean she could bend down and scoop up the phone.

A breeze gusted behind her, as if encouraging her inside. She peered hard at the black open doorway, trying to discern the shapes within it. There was a solid mass to the right. Was she looking at the coats hanging beside the front door?

The ticking of the central heating suddenly stopped.

Rose's fitful breathing seemed so loud now. Her eyes dipped to the phone and she bent her legs as her fingers reached for it.

A low scuffing noise.

She froze, attention zipping back to the doorway.

What she assumed to be the coats was moving, slowly but discernibly.

Rose waited a second longer, body rigid. *Pick up the phone.*

But the shape was moving faster. It was a figure and now there were footfalls under it.

Rose turned and leaped for the doorway, swivelling on her heel and sliding the door shut behind her. Her attention remained on the glass as her harsh breath partially clouded her view through the pane.

The figure was framed in the doorway but still in shadow. She held the door firmly in place. The phone lay between them. She should have just rushed in and grabbed it. She bent lower, poised to flee if she saw him cross the room.

But he remained where he was.

Rose felt an icy current pass through her. He was looking straight at her, watching the cloud of her breathing billowing on the glass. Any reflex to yell at the figure to get out of her home was suffocated by his static presence. Rose didn't want to blink but after what seemed like minutes had passed, she did. Briefly breaking contact with the outline melted it back into the oblong of shadow.

Now it looked like he had gone but she was sure he hadn't.

Was he waiting for her to try it again? She couldn't risk going back inside. She didn't want to release the door, but she had to get back to Noah. The only way out now was to try to scale the wall and raise the alarm.

Would he rush her as soon as she let go of the handle? She swallowed and heard it loud in both ears as she tried to spot movement through the doorway. *You're wasting time. Get Noah and push him over the wall.*

A few seconds later, Rose unstuck her palm from the handle and sucked in air as if doing so would trigger his emergence from the hallway.

No movement, no outline beyond.

She took one step back and wondered if he would wait for her to be clear of the door before he came through it. Another pace and a small choking noise escaped her.

'What are you doing?'

Rose didn't turn in the direction of the voice. 'Stay where you are,' she croaked.

'Why?' Noah replied loudly.

Rose bounced her open hand beside her to gesture for him to be quiet.

'Are you locked out?' Noah's voice was getting louder. He was walking up the lawn towards her.

'Stay there!' Her voice broke out this time.

'What's wrong?' There was trepidation in his.

She repeated the gesture, kept her eyes fixed on the door and took another step back. Another one and he could cross the lounge floor before she could put her weight back on the handle.

She could hear her son's light footfalls getting closer.

'Go to the back wall.' She said it loud and clear.

'What for?' he eventually replied, his voice small and frightened.

She didn't want to look away from the lounge. But she had to. Had to put her back to it. Rose peered one more time through her breath on the glass and then turned.

'Run!'

Chapter Twelve

She quickly caught up with Noah and put her hand on his back to propel him forward. He yelped as he pumped his arms, clearly aware that something was badly wrong. They passed the dimly glowing tent and the bay tree and then entered the pitch darkness at the end of the lawn. Low black clouds and the shadows of the overhanging trees made it impossible to see. Rose could feel every footfall thud in her chest.

'Who's after us?' Noah asked from her right.

Rose halted and gazed back at the double-glazed door. Nobody standing there. But perhaps he'd already opened it and was coming after them in the shadows. Was the door slid open? She squinted but it was difficult to tell from that distance. They were now about forty yards away.

'Is it a burglar?' Noah had stopped too.

She could smell her son's sour breath as it clouded up at her. 'Ssshhh!'

They both waited. Rose's circulation clamoured in her head as she tried to discern footsteps approaching. Perhaps the intruder was creeping stealthily down the lawn.

'I'm going to lift you over the wall,' she whispered and turned to touch the solid brick.

'It's too high,' he hissed back fearfully.

'No, it's not. Put your foot in my hand. I'll lift you as high up the wall as I can, and you scramble over the top.' She returned her attention to the house and the dark space between it and them.

'What about you?'

'You can pull me up,' she lied. How long would it take her to find the knife in the tent? 'Quick now, can you see my hands?' Rose interlinked her fingers, palms up, and put her right side against the cold mossy wall.

'I can't see.'

Rose could barely make out his outline. 'Come over here.' She put her right hand on his shoulder, guided him to where she was and then linked her fingers again. 'Put your foot here.'

Noah grunted as he did.

She took the weight of his rubber sole. 'I'll count three and you try to get a grip as far up as you can, OK?' She didn't wait for his reply. 'One, two… three!'

But Noah mistimed it and he wobbled and staggered back.

'Are you OK? Try again. On three, you stand up and I'll get you as high up as I can.' She took her position, glanced sideways towards the house. Still no sign of anyone at the door. 'Quickly.'

'It won't work. It's too high.'

'Do as I tell you.' But she suspected he was right. 'On three.'

He put his slipper in her hands again.

'One, two… three.'

This time they were in unison and Rose lifted his foot to chest height. She could hear his fingers scrabbling on the bricks.

'Grab a hold!'

His body swayed above her, but she turned and got her weight under his heel, driving him higher.

'There's nothing for me to hold onto!'

'Ssshhh!' Her shoulders shook with the exertion of holding him up. She wondered if the intruder was standing behind her, watching their escape attempt with amusement. She couldn't turn around.

'Let me down,' Noah pleaded, petrified.

'Just lie flat against the wall. I'll hold you there safe, I promise.' She couldn't maintain his bulk much longer. But Noah veered to the left, and she had to quickly adjust her footing. 'Lie against the wall.' She took hold of his other heel and tried to balance him, but his legs swayed in her grip. 'Open your arms wide… spread yourself against the wall.'

Noah let out an exclamation of frustration.

Rose managed to straighten him, but his legs still trembled and most of his weight was still in her palms. 'Just lean into the wall. I've got you.'

But he started to totter sideways. 'I'm falling!'

'Cling to the wall.' But she couldn't hold him up another second.

Noah collapsed to the right, and she heard him thud hard to the ground. He yelped in pain.

'Noah.' She turned around quickly to look back up at the house.

Nobody behind her.

'Noah?'

He didn't reply.

Chapter Thirteen

Rose crouched to the ground. 'Answer me.' She extended her hand, touched his face. It felt hot. 'Are you OK?'

Noah groaned. 'I've hurt my shoulder.'

'Ssshhh.' She still couldn't hear anyone else on the lawn. 'We have to try again.'

Noah attempted to rise but gasped.

Rose's eyes scoured the lit windows of the house. She couldn't see any sign of the intruder. 'Come on. We nearly did it.' She stood with him.

'It's too high.'

'It's our only way out. We can't go through the house.'

'Maybe you scared them away.'

Rose wanted to believe that, but as she studied the windows through their clouds of breath, she didn't want to waste any time speculating. 'Let's try again.'

'My shoulder really hurts.'

'You'll be OK. Step into my hand.'

But Noah didn't.

'Quickly.'

'I can't feel my arm.'

Rose ran her hand gently down his right shoulder. 'This one?'

He replied by flinching and sucking in his breath.

'You don't think you can climb?'

'No.'

She felt him wince again. 'OK.' She tried to steady her breathing. 'OK…' What else could they do? Even if she could scale the wall, she wouldn't be able to lift Noah up by his arms. 'Let's think.'

'I'm sorry.'

'Don't be silly. You did your best.'

A sliding noise.

Both of them froze.

It was nearby.

'That was the sound,' Noah whispered.

'Quiet.' Rose looked around for a weapon. Wasn't there an old spade around here? There was a faint glow of a broken white stoneware pot lying on the border to her right. She picked it up and shook out the earth inside.

'It was over there.'

Rose knew exactly where. The movement had been somewhere on the border to their left. Had the intruder followed them down and been biding his time while they proved they couldn't escape?

The noise came again. A low dragging.

'That was even nearer.' Noah retreated against her. 'I wish I hadn't left my penlight in the tent.'

The sound increased in volume but stopped abruptly.

They were both motionless.

It had been very close, but Rose still couldn't see any movement in front of them. 'If you leave now, I won't call the police!'

Rose and Noah waited for a response.

'I've got a knife,' she lied. 'I'll do anything to protect my son.' She felt Noah's head turn towards her and put her hand over his mouth. 'Any closer and I'll use it.'

But the dragging got nearer.

Rose moved Noah behind her and brandished the broken pot in readiness.

Chapter Fourteen

'Hold on to me and move this way,' Rose said, barely above a whisper, and took a pace to her right. Noah stepped with her.

The noise stopped.

She remained rooted to the spot and clenched the broken pot harder.

The sound came again.

Rose slid them towards the right wall, manoeuvring them away from whatever was on their left. Could the intruder see them or were she and Noah just as hidden in shadow as he was?

The dragging stopped.

So did she. Noah froze beside her.

Seconds passed but there was no further activity from the other side of the lawn.

Rose looked back at the house. If the intruder was close,

should they now make a break for it? They could run in through the lounge, grab the phone and head straight out the front door. Would the intruder catch up to them before they'd unlocked it though? Even if they got out of the house and called the police, there was still over a mile of road before they reached the village. Rose thought about how they could run behind the bus shelter past the footbridge and try to lose themselves in the undergrowth there.

She continued to sidle them gradually along the border and estimated they were drawing close to being opposite the source of the movement. The dimly lit tent was between them and the house. Rose slid her foot out to the right and felt the smooth lawn with the sole of her slipper before gradually shifting her weight to it. The closer they got to the house, the more chance they had of getting out through the front drive and getting a head start.

The noise started again ahead of them. Closer than it had been before.

Rose was screaming but holding it inside. She crouched low, bringing Noah with her.

The bay tree rustled in the wind as if to confirm its presence, but the sounds drowned out the others she was straining to hear. Rose gripped the fragment of the pot so it almost cut into her palm.

The wind eventually died, and it was quiet again.

Rose could feel Noah breathing against the side of her face as they waited.

A police siren echoed far away and then vanished.

Rose wondered where it was going. It was no help to them. They had to rescue themselves. As soon as they got near the house, they would be in the light spilling from the windows and that's when they'd have to run. *Go now.*

They moved together, Noah's footsteps treading gently after hers.

Her attention was on the closed lounge window as she and Noah encroached on the weak edge of light at the patio. The door was closed and there was nobody in the room. Her eyes flitted about the other windows. No sign of the figure. The intruder had to be somewhere on the lawn.

The dragging noise came again but this time it was muted. Further behind them.

As soon as they stepped near the sliding doors, they'd be visible. She squinted through the window at the doorway to the hall. Nobody was standing there. How could they be? The intruder was out there with them. But she hadn't heard the door rattle open and shut again. She'd been running with Noah, but surely, she would have heard it. Maybe he was still waiting inside. Rose listened for the sound again.

Nothing.

Had it been an animal in the forest? Noah had heard it earlier and the intruder could already have been inside the house then. What the hell should they do? Go inside where the intruder could still be waiting because he knew she and Noah would never scale the walls, or stay put when he could be hiding behind them in the shadows?

'Let's go in,' Noah whispered.

She realised his whole body was trembling. So was hers. But they couldn't loiter here.

At that moment the lawn was suddenly bathed in blue light. A cloud had shifted and the moon illuminated the whole area.

There was nobody else in sight.

The dragging noise came, loud but brief.

Noah gripped her waist tighter.

Still no sign of where the activity was coming from.

They were quite alone. The sound had to be coming from the forest.

'What is that?' Noah's voice quaked.

'Ssshhh. If they're still in the house, they'll know exactly where we are.' Her focus was on the lounge again. Rose felt a stab of relief that he wasn't hiding in the dark out here, but it meant they were still stuck. 'Follow me to the other side.'

'Why?'

'Quickly. Take my hand.'

Noah gripped it firmly.

Rose led him to the wall opposite 'Look, this part of the wall has lost a layer of bricks at the top. It's the shortest section to climb. Try scaling it again while I keep watch.'

'I can't. My shoulder really hurts.'

'I'll be right behind you. If we can get out into the forest, we can climb over the fence onto the road. You'll have to put up with a little pain, but I know we can do it. You go

first and I'll push you up as much as I can. Start climbing.'
Rose turned back to the house. Still no movement in the lounge.

Noah grunted as he started to scale it.

'OK?'

'I've got a foothold.'

'See how far up you can get. Then I'll give you a boost.'

Rose squinted at the double-glazed door again. Where was her phone? She couldn't see it lying on the floor. She took a few paces towards the house to confirm its absence.

A muffled grunt from behind her.

Rose turned. 'Noah?'

He was no longer on the wall.

Rose's eyes dropped to the edge of the lawn.

Noah was there but only half of him was visible. His legs were under the earth. She could see the back of his head. Two bare adult arms were protruding from under the dirt, covering his mouth. They couldn't conceal his scream though. It was guttural – pure terror.

And then Noah was swiftly dragged out of sight and under the ground.

Chapter Fifteen

Something primal exploded from Rose, half her son's name and half a reaction to his disappearance into the hole. She was on her knees, hands delving into the mud as it sunk and filled in the opening that had swallowed him. She was up to her wrists, fingers frantically scooping the wet soil.

She felt the ground giving under her knees and tipped forward. Rose was sinking too. She dropped down hard, the sides of the trench suddenly muffling everything but her harsh panting. She was about four feet below where she'd been stood but kept digging into the dark fragments in front of her. 'Noah!'

His muffled yell was quickly cut short.

Was that behind or in front of her? She froze for a few seconds, but the only sound was the channels of earth pouring into where she was crouching. 'Noah!'

This time he didn't respond.

Rose started paddling her hands. She could feel the weight of the dirt streaming onto her head. It was in her mouth as she clawed at the thicker clay and tangled roots.

She crawled ahead another couple of feet but the trench in front of her had filled with crumbling mud.

Noah yelped as if he were in pain.

That was behind her. She tried to turn in the confined space but couldn't.

It was suddenly black; a heavy load pressed her shoulders down hard. She couldn't lift herself back up. She'd been buried. Rose could feel her heart thudding in her ears. *Get up!*

But even as she exerted her stomach muscles and tried to rise, she couldn't even lift her head.

A dull hissing sound. The trench wall had caved in on her. More soil was piling on top of it.

Noah's down here as well. Rose's chin was resting painfully against her fingers. She pushed hard at the wet floor beneath her.

The bulk pinning her down was getting heavier.

She dug the heels of her hands hard into the earth and took all her weight in them. Her shoulder lifted an inch but the pressure pushed her back down. *If you don't get up now, you never will.*

Rose's whole frame trembled as she attempted to rise further. She could taste the earth, her teeth grinding it as she strained every sinew in her upper torso to try and punch through the layer of dirt above her.

She raised another half an inch, breathed in the soil through her nose. Her circulation hammered as she grunted and used her knees to lever herself up.

The mud started to give, but the weight bore down as more of it slid into the trench. Rose pressed the crown of her head against it and drove herself hard behind it.

Her scream broke her through and suddenly the cold air was on her face again. But more earth was falling on her scalp, threatening to bury her again. She waggled her shoulders from side to side, twisted her body as she fought to get free.

Rose pulled her right hand up and got it clear. Then the other. Quickly heaving herself out, she turned around on the pile of collapsed dirt and started digging in the opposite direction. 'Noah, answer me!' She spat out mud and ploughed at the large mound blocking the channel.

For the first time, she began to ask herself exactly what she was crawling through. The sides were flat, like it had been dug out. How far back to the house did it extend? She slid forward and downwards on her knees again. Her hands raked at the cascading soil, but it was flowing in quicker than she could burrow through it. 'Answer me!'

She waited, tried to discern any cries but the torrent of earth was creating an ever-deeper barrier between them. 'Noah!'

As if to compound her powerlessness, another huge chunk slid into the channel and trapped her hands underneath it.

Rose tried to yank them out as another side of the trench slumped on top of her.

Chapter Sixteen

R ose didn't want to relinquish her position in the trench but as more of it disintegrated, she knew she might not be able to pull herself free a second time. She painfully jerked out her hands, grabbed the edges of the chunk that had fallen and used it to step on before hauling herself up. It crumbled as she put her weight on it and her body slid back as it broke apart. Digging her nails hard into the clay wall, she dragged herself into the cool night and lugged herself over the edge.

For seconds, her breath burst from her in clouds, but she quickly scrambled to her feet.

Most of the trench had filled with dirt now but there had to be an exit. As her chest heaved, she squinted along the wall back to the house. As far as she knew, the intruder hadn't come outside. Had he crawled through a tunnel from inside? It must have been what the dragging noise had been. Somebody had been underneath them.

She staggered along the wall, searching for further signs of collapse. But the dead flowers were undisturbed. She halted and considered trying to scale the wall. Perhaps the tunnel started on the other side. But the intruder had definitely been inside the house. *The cellar.*

Rose reached the patio but slowed as she approached the doors. Still no sign of anyone in the lounge. And her phone had definitely been removed. The landline had been disconnected five weeks ago. That iPhone was her only way to call the police. What about her laptop? It had been on the packing case with Noah's. Only the pizza box was there now.

She couldn't afford to hesitate. Rose gripped the handle and depressed it softly.

It clicked loudly as the door was released. Wincing, she rattled it back as quietly as she could on the runner.

Go to the kitchen. There are still a couple of other bigger knives in the drawer. Grab one and go down to the cellar.

The notion of Noah being dragged there tugged away her fear and Rose stepped into the lounge, her attention on the doorway to the hall. She paused at the threshold, listening for sounds from the cellar.

Silence.

Rose breathed in unevenly, stole quickly into the room and padded purposefully down the passage of boxes to the kitchen. She pulled the drawer harder than she wanted and the contents clattered loudly. She blenched but it was pointless trying to conceal her presence. She had to fight for Noah now.

Rose took out the largest blade. It was the bread knife.

Again, she paused to listen, trapping her breath in her chest.

Nothing. The heating had turned off for the night.

She gripped the handle of the knife, raised it to shoulder height and returned the way she'd come.

The lounge ahead was still empty, but she immediately crossed the wooden floor and flicked on the remaining switches beside the open door.

She stood back as the hallway was illuminated. Empty. The chain was still across the front door, so nobody had entered or left that way.

Had she been wrong? Maybe the tunnel did lead somewhere else. Or had the mud collapsed in on both of them and they were lying under a ton of earth?

Momentarily, Rose hovered where she was, indecision locking her limbs.

Get a spade. Dig them out.

All the tools from the garage were packed. But wasn't there an old one at the end of the lawn somewhere?

Check the cellar first. It's on the same level as the trench.

Noah had helped her carry up the last of the boxes from there that day. It was completely empty now.

Rose stepped into the hallway and turned right to where

the door was at the end of the stair panels. Light illuminated the crack around the closed door.

She remembered turning it off when they'd brought the last crate up. She remembered because as she'd flicked the switch and sealed the dark, wood panelled door, she'd wondered if it was the last time she'd ever go down there. And now she knew the answer.

Find Noah.

Her knuckles tightened, turning white on the knife. She put her fingers out to the handle.

'Rose?' The muffled male voice from behind it called out as casually as Lucas would have. Like he needed her help with some minor chore. 'Rose, can you come down here a moment?'

Why did she recognise it?

Chapter Seventeen

Don't go down there, an internal voice screamed. *Get to Noah*. Her maternal instinct overrode everything else. Her fingertips were frozen inches away from the door handle. Whoever it was knew she was standing there; had probably heard her movement in and out of the kitchen from down in the cellar. She opened her mouth, but she didn't know how to respond. How did he know her name?

'Rose?' There was light-hearted remonstration in his tone.

'Noah!' His name burst from her.

No response from behind the door.

'Noah, are you down there?' Rose's leg trembled as she anticipated footsteps up the wooden stairs.

None came.

Maybe he was already standing at the top. But his voice

didn't sound close enough. Her hand was still wavering at the handle.

'Rose…' There was more censure behind the word.

She took a step back. That sounded closer. Was he standing at the bottom of the stairs?

'Where's Noah?' she demanded.

'He's down here,' he eventually replied. 'With me.' His tone was conciliatory, as if it were a situation to be expected.

She *did* know the voice. But where from? 'Noah, answer me.'

Still nothing.

'Where is he!'

'I've told you.' But it was good-tempered irritation.

'Noah!'

'What did you just get out of the drawer, Rose?'

She lowered the blade, as if he could see it.

'If I'm brutally honest, I've had better receptions.'

'Just let him go. I won't call the police. I promise.'

'And I know you'll be as good as your word. I've confiscated your phone and laptops and your landline was disconnected last month.'

The genial way he informed her settled cold on Rose's shoulders. How did he know?

'Open the door and come down,' he invited.

'Let him go. Please.' But she guessed that begging wasn't going to appease him. 'My husband is due home any moment.'

'If I had a penny every time I heard that…' There was a chuckle in his reply. 'D'you know how much I'd have?'

'He's due home. And I've got another phone up here. I'll call the police first.'

'Five pennies.'

A tiny creak from below.

Rose took a step back. Was he creeping up the stairs?

'Just let him go!' She hadn't heard a sound from Noah.

'Go ahead, call the police. I'll wait here while you do it,' he called up breezily. 'There's an old dartboard here. I can occupy myself for a few minutes.'

Should she continue her bluff? He already knew she was lying.

The sound of a dart thudding into the board made her jump.

'You've got until I throw a triple twenty, which, given my mediocre ability, could mean you've got all night.'

Another thud.

'Go ahead if that's something that makes you more comfortable.'

'What do you want!'

'I've already told you.'

A third thud.

'Well, look at that. I'm better at this than I remember.'

Chapter Eighteen

'Time's up, Rose!'

Again, she wondered how he knew her name. This wasn't a random break-in. Did he also know for sure that Lucas wouldn't be coming home?

Silence hung between them.

'And there's nothing else to keep me out of trouble down here!'

Noah screamed.

Rose felt it resonate in her core. His voice was muffled and distant. 'Noah!'

Noah shouted back but the words were garbled.

'Noah, are you all right!' Had it come from the cellar? It didn't sound close enough. Where was he?

'There's nothing I'd like more than to reunite the two of you, but if we're to get that underway, you're going to have to join me down here.'

'Noah! Can you hear me?'

Again Noah responded, but his words were frantic and incoherent.

Rose waited for him to stop. 'Noah, listen to me…' She had to pacify him. 'I'm right here. OK?' A bubble of fear was expanding in her throat. 'I'm coming to get you.'

More panicked and incomprehensible words poured from him.

'Let him go!' she screamed at the cellar door.

'At the risk of pointing out the obvious, this is clearly a time-sensitive scenario, Rose. What do you say?'

What choice did she have? But it didn't sound as if Noah was in the same room as the intruder. Perhaps he was still inside the trench. The notion of him being trapped underground swept through her like nausea. 'Do what you want to me, but please let him go!'

Her words rung around the empty house.

Was that what he wanted? In that instant, Rose knew she would do anything to release Noah. Subject herself to any ordeal to free him.

'It's a very kind gesture, Rose. And it's the sort of hospitality I've grown accustomed to. But at the moment, all I want is your presence. So, if we're in agreement that neither the police nor Lucas are coming…'

She hadn't mentioned his name. He knew too much about them. 'Who are you?'

'I'd say that *what* I am is more relevant at the moment. And that is tired, dirty and inconvenienced.' He was still buoyant but exhaled. 'And I really don't want to add impatient to the list.'

Rose heard him walk a few paces back and forth on the concrete floor of the cellar.

'And as soon as you lose patience, you lose control. So why don't we have a calm, adult discussion about the predicament we find ourselves in?'

She transferred her weigh onto her trembling leg.

Noah howled. The harrowing, mournful sound seeming to punctuate the inevitability of what had to happen next.

'Rose? Are you still there?'

'I'm here,' she replied flatly. Rose felt the bubble swell in her throat and the blood pumping unsteadily through her eardrums as she reached out and tugged the handle. The door opened and she could see down the stairs to a small section of the dirty grey floor below.

From her angle, she could just see the tips of the intruder's boots as he waited for her.

Chapter Nineteen

'Were you thinking of making us some sandwiches?'

Rose's gaze switched briefly to the bread knife clutched securely in her fist, the blade below the heel of her hand. As she tentatively descended each stair, more of the intruder became visible. Whatever image she had of the voice's owner seemed to be negated by every step.

After a pair of muddy black boots, she saw their dirty navy jeans. A hairy paunch hung over them and soon she was looking at the bottle-green T-shirt that seemed too tight for his chest. It was caked with mud as well as his bare arms.

Finally, his face came into view and she recalled exactly who he was. He was one of the middle-aged men who had been working for Ty Maynard. He'd been in the house that afternoon. His head was sitting on a thick neck and the greying dark hair was closely shaved to a stepped fine sheen on his scalp. He looked to be mid to late fifties. His gaze was heavily lidded, but the pale blue eyes that fixed her were piercing. They were the sharpest thing within his smudgy features. His nose was broad and upper lip pronounced. There was a ring that pierced his septum and hung down from his nostrils that added to his bovine appearance, along with several other rings hanging from each earlobe. A streak of dirt bisected his face.

'Just hang fire there.' He held out a pudgy and muddy palm.

His voice seemed miniature in relation to his frame, as if someone were throwing their voice into him. Rose halted on the bottom stair.

'What the hell are you doing here?' He hadn't said a word to her that afternoon. She recalled making him a cup of coffee and him accepting it from her without a word of thanks. She'd heard him speaking to the other men though.

'Seems a little… antisocial.' He nodded at the blade.

Rose's fist shook as if she were steadying her whole body around the knife handle.

'Where is he?' she blurted, her eyes quickly darting about the empty cellar. No sign of Noah.

'Come in, help yourself to dips. You're skipping all that and going straight to assault with a deadly weapon?' His unkempt and wiry dark eyebrows lifted and revealed the humour in his eyes.

'Give him to me.' The tightening in her chest barely let

her release the words. 'We'll walk out of here, and you can take whatever you want.'

'That's very kind but there's nothing you can give me that isn't already mine.' His eyebrows dropped, his expression set and assured.

Rose tried to swallow. He was deliberately allowing her to absorb what the words meant. He appeared completely calm. He raised his other hand and showed her his empty palm. 'I don't have a weapon. I'm not threatening you. Can we both sing from the same hymn sheet?' He looked pointedly at the knife.

Rose shook her head once.

'OK. You hold onto that for a moment,' he placated. 'I'll give you some space.' He took three very deliberate steps backwards.

She knew why he was so confident that she wouldn't attack him. He had Noah. And she was terrified. He didn't need a weapon. 'I did… as you asked.' The words pumped out. 'Give him to me. Please.'

'See that?' His eyes jinked left.

Hers did too. Three darts were in the board. She returned her gaze to his.

'Triple twenty on my third throw. This is definitely my night. That's maybe something you should take on board.'

As she clenched the knife, she could feel her circulation pound in her wrist.

'Do you ever do that thing – this one's for my life?'

When she could see he was waiting for a response, she shook her head again.

'You should try it. When it's the shot that really matters, you just say to yourself, "This one's for my life." You've never done that?' He seemed genuinely surprised.

Rose managed to gulp and breathe in unevenly.

'That's what I did with that dart. You're leaving that board behind?'

She nodded.

'Noah not a player?'

'Let him go.' She brandished the knife but knew it was futile.

'I will. I promise.' He raised both grubby palms. 'There's a lot of stuff I need to do first though.'

As he shifted his footing, his body moved slightly right, and Rose could see the white painted wall behind him. There was a dark hole there about four feet wide, the bricks collapsed inside. A few lay on the floor in front of it.

The intruder let her take it in.

'Haden Bloom.' He studied her frown. 'I know your name. Only fair you know mine.' Extending his hand, he took a pace forward.

Rose stepped back up a stair.

He halted, withdrew his arm and put it behind his back. 'OK. Moving too fast. I do want to be done here by morning though. I've got an appointment with my chiropractor at 10.30 and it's virtually impossible to reschedule.' He blinked and cocked his head at her as he awaited her reply.

'Where is Noah?' It felt like the bottom half of her body would give way.

He stood more to one side and nodded at the opening.

'Noah!' she called into it.

Bloom raised his wiry eyebrows again and rolled his eyeballs up as he anticipated an answer.

Noah's voice yelled back but it was now obvious that he was trying to shout through a gag.

'This is the only way in. Knew I'd need to take the plasterboard back off at some stage, so I bricked it up loose. I love the new kitchen layout, by the way.' His eyes briefly tilted to the ceiling of the cellar.

Rose tried to process what he'd said.

'When I lived here, I never got that right, but you've nailed it. Plenty of storage and a station for prep and plating up. I hope whoever's bought this place appreciates that.'

Noah screamed again.

'I'm here! I'm coming to get you!' *Stab him now.*

'I've always kept an interest in this place. I didn't really want to leave, if I'm honest. It was a rental property then and they jacked up the rent. Sky high. Just so they could get rid of me and sell it. I knew I was giving up the nearest thing I've ever had to a real home. How long were you and your husband here? Actually, I know that. I'm just wondering why you decided to leave after seven years. Purely financial?'

Rose realized her mouth was half open. His incongruous

conversation was so out of synch with the jeopardy of the situation, but she didn't doubt the threat he presented.

'You bought from the Drews, didn't you?'

She nodded once.

'Seemed like a nice couple but they were the third people to flip the place. Still, good news for you. Are you selling up because Lucas's care is so costly?'

Rose felt a rock of dread drop into her stomach. He knew Lucas was never coming home.

'Nobody stays here long. The O'Briens less than a year, the Millers six months, and the Drews about nine months. You're the longest since me. Were you as attached to the place as I was?'

Run at him. Plant the knife deep in his belly. While he's not expecting it. While you've still got a chance.

Bloom cocked his head to the right as if he were listening to her thoughts. 'You've gone quiet.'

Noah was saying something from behind him, but his voice was weaker, more imploring.

Was he suffocating? Rose tensed her legs.

'You look overwrought, Rose. Don't let us get off on the wrong foot.'

He knows what you're about to do. But now could be your only chance.

Rose launched herself from the stairs.

Chapter Twenty-One

Suddenly Bloom's impassive face was filling her vision and pain was jolting the left side of her body. She cried out as she folded and her knees struck the concrete. His legs were in front of her. Before she could pull her arm back to stab him in the crotch, however, her right wrist was twisted hard.

'Let it go. I'll tell you once.'

She didn't and screamed again. It felt like her wrist was about to break.

'You're all Noah's got, all that's standing between him and me.'

She could feel his other fingers digging hard into her left shoulder while his hand maintained the pressure on her wrist.

'Your maternal instincts are flawless but you're overestimating what you're capable of, Rose. Drop it.'

She kept her hold on the blade but when she tried to free herself, he increased the pressure on her shoulder and wrist. She tried to stand up, but he drove her back down.

'You tried. You can take comfort from that.' Bloom hadn't altered his tone. 'But you're more use to Noah as you are now.'

She could smell him now: a Savlon or Vaseline aroma and a vague undercurrent of his cheap cologne. She still held onto the knife.

'I want you intact. You'll need both hands.' His breathing hadn't even quickened.

'Let us go,' she said through gritted teeth.

'I don't have time for this.' He deftly twisted her wrist the wrong way.

Rose screamed and after the flash of agony, she realised she'd dropped the knife.

Bloom scraped it up and took a pace back.

Rose sprang to her feet, cradling her aching hand. She could still feel the indentations throbbing where his fingers had dug between the bones of her left shoulder.

'You can come at me again, if you want.' Bloom reversed the blade so the handle was extended to her. 'I think you're smarter than that though. And I think Noah's time is even more precious than mine.' He held her in his beady gaze and tilted his head to one side.

Rose's chest heaved.

'Serrated blades are better for disposal. Not dispatch. I

appreciate you're working with what you've got but this would make things very messy for both of us. Do me the courtesy of sparing us that.'

She blinked moisture out of her eyes as she briefly regarded the weapon he was offering back to her. He'd effortlessly repelled her attack. But would she get another chance?

'That would be option one. Option two is a no-brainer. Option two is climbing in there.' He cocked his head at the opening in the wall.

Rose flinched as she tried to flex the fingers of her injured right hand.

She frowned.

'That's exactly where you want to go, isn't it? Find Noah. Set him free.'

Rose looked down at the blade again.

'If I really wanted to harm you, I could already have done that. I could be home and tucked up in bed by now. I could even use this knife on you right now, couldn't I? This knife you so helpfully carried down here for me.'

She raised her eyes to his.

'How's that hand?'

She balled it into a fist.

'Working order. You'll probably need some ice on it, but you can soldier on.'

Snatch the knife. Take it from him and stick it in his stomach. There's enough to aim for. But she suspected he would either whip it from her reach or do the same to her again as soon as she tried to use it.

'It's your lucky night. If you threw a dart at the board, I think you'd get a triple twenty too. Fact is, tonight, I really need your help. What d'you say, Rose?'

Chapter Twenty-Two

Noah's distress echoed out of the wall again.

'Just try to stay calm! Are you hurt?' she called back. 'Is he hurt?' Rose pointedly addressed Bloom.

'No. I don't think so. Understandably alarmed. It's pretty dark and filthy in there.' He gently pricked the palm of his hand with the blade of the bread knife.

'You can't gag Noah. Noah has asthma and needs his inhaler. It's back in the tent. Noah has to have his inhaler.' She reminded herself to use his name as often as possible.

'Noah's inhaler stays in Noah's tent and doesn't get mentioned again. Unless you want me to break Noah's inhaler. You seem determined to break his name. Don't worry, he can breathe OK. When I bound him, I was more than careful not to cut off the blood supply to his wrists and ankles.'

Was that meant to mitigate what he'd done? Rose felt sick to her stomach as she thought of Noah being tied up by Bloom in the dark. 'I'm coming to get you!'

Noah didn't respond.

'Noah!' She moved away from Bloom towards the hole.

Bloom stepped back a pace.

Rose kept one eye on his position. 'Answer me!'

He did but again it was unintelligible. His voice sounded weaker.

'You can find him, if you like.'

She turned to Bloom, knowing it wasn't going to be as simple as that.

'I spent long evenings in there.' He pointed with the blade to the hole. 'Noah is in one of the tunnels that I dug out over a period of five years. There are three, all running under this house as well as the rear lawn. They represent a lot of toil and sweat on my part,' he said with some pride.

Rose gazed into the pitch-black opening in front of her.

'But the supports aren't as sturdy as they were. You saw how easily tunnel three collapsed. Guess the house has sunk and the earth has shifted since I last lived here.'

'Please, bring him out of there. We'll both stay down here in the cellar. We won't try anything and you can do whatever you need to do.'

'But the walls aren't the only thing to sag since then.' He rubbed his free hand under his protruding belly. 'Too many carbs and not enough exercise.'

Rose's wrist smarted and she flinched.

'I've become... what's that term for overweight and lazy? "Contented".'

She shifted a step closer to the hole. Should she crawl in there? She could move faster than him. Was there another exit or, even if she found Noah, would they both have to escape back through this hole where he'd be waiting for them?

'I'm not the person I was when I lived here. I was so focused then. Didn't need the afternoon naps. Scarcely slept, in fact. Just me in there for hours. Whole weekends sometimes.' He sounded nostalgic.

Why? Was that the question he wanted her to ask? But she already dreaded the answer.

'Three tunnels but not interconnected.' He nodded at the hole. 'You can access one–three that way but there's no lighting in there.'

She knew exactly why he was telling her. 'Why did you dig them?' she asked, trying to keep her voice steady.

'It's where I keep my luggage.' He let her absorb that. 'Feel free to escape that way, Rose. But if you go crawling down a wrong turn, you're not going to find Noah.'

Rose opened her mouth to call to Noah again, but his name remained in her throat.

'The air's very thin in there. Not the best conditions for someone with breathing issues.'

She shook her head. Was he getting off on frightening

her or was he right about her getting lost in there? And if she did, what would happen to Noah?

'And he just might stumble on some of my luggage as well.'

Chapter Twenty-Three

Rose turned to face him. She knew how much he wanted her to ask the question. 'What luggage?'

'There are four suitcases in there. I'm not exactly in tip-top shape so it's going to be pretty hard crawling in and dragging them out myself. You clearly look after yourself though.' He regarded her physique.

She guessed why.

'Having an energetic nine-year-old to run around after helps. Am I right?'

Rose tried to recall if she'd mentioned Noah's age when the removal men had been in the house earlier. He knew everything about them.

'What's in the cases?' The end of her question was cut off as her mouth dried.

'The real question is about time. Do you have any inkling who you're selling to?'

Rose frowned. 'The Campbells?'

'That's right. The foster parents. At least, that's the story they fed you but it's a classic piece of emotional deception. The Campbells actually work for Spear Cosmetics. This is the third piece of rural property and land they've secured for them in the last two years and the company intend to redevelop it.'

Rose could barely focus on what he was saying to her.

'You may have noticed Spear Cosmetics has been all over the news recently. They have quite a cavalier attitude towards animal testing and vivisection. That's why they like these obscure tucked-away locations.' He waited for her reaction.

Rose's attention was still on the hole but now she started to digest his words.

'Means it's a long hike for animal activists... when they eventually realise they've pitched camp here,' he said with his contained voice.

Rose shook her head. What did this have to do with their predicament?

'What Spear does is of no consequence to me, but I do know that redevelopment will mean this whole area is about to be churned up. I can't have them finding my luggage. What's inside each one is of exceptional value to me. I want them out of here as soon as possible, but you'll understand why I couldn't exactly bring in my boss's removals company. I've worked for Ty Maynard for seven years now and it's given me access to a lot of these local isolated properties. We actually shifted the furniture for the last three families who lived here but I'm always diligent about background checking the next residents. This place has sentimental value to me. I have to know it's in good hands and that I'm the only person who knows what's behind that wall.' He gestured to the collapsed bricks. 'After a bit of research on the Campbells, alarm bells sounded.'

She turned back to the hole. 'Noah!'

His muted voice groaned.

'He's fine. I dragged him clear before tunnel three completely collapsed. He's safe and tucked away but you'll be taking pot luck if you crawl in there without me giving you directions.'

'Just hold on. I'm coming!' Should she believe him or could she find Noah alone? Regardless, they still had to get out of the cellar.

'I would give you a few minutes to think about it, but I don't think you have them. What d'you say? Retrieve four cases for me and I point you to Noah. I'll tell you exactly where they are. My removal van's parked up nearby so I'll need you to help me load it. Then I'm gone.' He raised his eyebrows, cocked his head to one side and blinked at her while he awaited her decision.

A fat-necked pigeon. That's what he reminded her of. But she sensed that his disarming persona concealed someone calculating and dangerous. Even after her attempt to stab him, he was still one hundred per cent calm. He'd been in these situations before. He was confident he could handle her. But maybe that was what she could use against him.

He had the knife now though, and even when he didn't, he seemed confident in her inability to harm him. Noah had to be her priority. 'OK. I want Noah out of there now.'

He remained tight-lipped, regarding her as if the demand didn't deserve a response.

'I have to know he's all right.'

'You'll be able to call to him when you're in there. I'll direct you to each tunnel and you'll find him in the tunnel where the last suitcase is,' he said matter-of-factly, as if the task was insignificant.

'And how do I know you'll let us go?'

'Why wouldn't I? You wouldn't think about speaking to anyone about our transaction?'

She shook her head once. But she'd seen his face. He'd given her his name.

'And I told you, I'll need your help loading up my van. That won't be a sciatica-friendly job. Don't underestimate your value to me.'

But that was probably a lie to give her hope. 'How heavy are the suitcases?'

He nodded, as if it were a constructive question. 'You'll be able to shift them. No heavier than anything you've lifted off a carousel. The only difficulty you might have is dragging them through the tighter parts of the tunnel. I got them in there though. You should be able to get them out.'

'Tell me what's inside them.'

'Is that something you absolutely need to know?' His eyes stopped blinking.

'Anything... breakable I mean?' But she'd caught his implication. The less she knew, the better. But she knew too much already.

'No. Nothing breakable. No kid gloves needed, just some good old-fashioned back work.'

'And what if I refuse?' Rose figured the answer, but she had to ask. Had to know if he was as much a threat to Noah as she believed. It felt like her circulation was briefly suspended.

'You can walk out of here now if you want. Run down the road, raise the alarm, call the police. I won't stop you.'

Rose doubted that.

'Whatever time you take to do that, though, will mean there'll be nobody here when you get back. Not me, not Noah.' He glanced at his watch and sniffed, his eyes on the beamed ceiling, as if he didn't want to look at her for having made him issue the threat. 'And *that* is the most palatable way I can think of to say it.'

Chapter Twenty-Four

'Any other questions?' He didn't meet her eye. The blade of the bread knife rested on his palm again.

Rose said nothing and considered the only option that was open to her. Bloom needed the cases, and she had the time it took to fetch four of them to figure out an escape plan.

'And just so you know, this is the only exit. Every tunnel is a dead end. You'll know when you get there because that's where you'll find each case. There are two stacked up in tunnel three.'

Rose turned to the hole in the wall. 'Noah! I'm coming to get you!'

Another inaudible response.

'I can hear you, but I can't understand what you're saying! Just stay calm and I'll be right there!'

'No time to waste then.' Bloom slid his eyes to the opening.

Was the whole story about suitcases a ploy? Did he plan to seal them both inside as soon as she crawled in? He was right though. He could have killed her with her own knife if he wanted.

'It's a little tight in places but you should be able to wriggle comfortably through. Some of the struts are rotten now so try not to disturb them. You don't want a cave-in.' He registered her reaction. 'I broke through the ceiling to the lawn but didn't expect the end section to collapse like that. That was my fault. And to be honest, it's more than a little shaken me. Someone your size should be fine though.'

Fine to be buried alive. Rose took a breath, walked forward and touched the damp brick edges of the hole with her palms. The blackness beyond was deep and solid and frigid air blew against her face. She could smell the earth.

'If there should be any accidents, though, remember I'm the only person who knows where you both are. You're relying on me to get you out.'

Which was another reason why she shouldn't be going inside but Rose had to get to Noah. And, as a past resident, Bloom clearly didn't want a discovery of whatever was in those tunnels to incriminate him. Right now, he needed her alive.

'Breathe slowly. Don't use up your oxygen. We don't want you passing out in there.'

Rose couldn't take another step forward but felt as if the

darkness was coming out of the hole to meet her. A fizzing sensation swept cold over her shoulders and up to her scalp.

'There's a lantern inside at your feet.'

Rose reached down into the darkness around her slippers and waved her fingers around. They came into contact with cold plastic and she picked up the lightweight object.

A phone rang.

Rose turned as she recognised her ring tone.

Bloom was standing behind her, his face expectant, with no indication that he was hearing her phone.

The sound was so close, it had to be in his pocket.

The phone kept ringing.

'They can leave a message.' He nodded for her to continue.

Who was calling her? Only a few feet away was a chance to cry for help. One button to press before someone knew exactly what was happening to her.

'It's an LED lantern. Switch is on the bottom. It's a little temperamental though. Just tap it lightly if it flickers.'

But the phone might as well be upstairs. It was in his pocket and he had the knife.

'You'll see three openings. Take the middle one. It's the narrowest. Let's get you acclimated with that one. If you're OK in there, the rest will be easy.' He had to talk louder over the ringing.

Her eyes dropped to the knife. He was pointing the blade towards her belly.

The phone rang and echoed down the tunnel behind her.

'Shout back when you've found the first case.'

Rose hovered there. Would she and Noah ever come out again?

The ringing stopped.

She exhaled and turned back to the hole. Clicking on the lantern, she pointed it ahead.

Chapter Twenty-Five

The circle of light revealed she was standing in a small antechamber a couple of feet deep. In front of her were three tunnels at waist height. The diameter of each was about four feet and just wide enough for an adult to crawl into.

'Use your elbows to pull yourself along,' he advised.

She spun back to him, but he hadn't moved any closer.

'You're wasting time.' He cocked his head again, his face impassive.

Rose turned back to the three openings and moved her lantern so it illuminated their uneven edges. 'How long are they?' she thought out loud, her voice hoarse.

'Some longer than others. Middle one is the shortest. Should only take you a couple of minutes to slither to the end.'

'Noah!' Her cry sounded flat inside the enclosed space.

He shouted back and it sounded like he was yelling through his nose.

Which tunnel had it come from? It was impossible to tell. Had to be one of the tunnels either side of the one Bloom was directing her into.

'I hope you're not wearing your best nightclothes.'

She hadn't even considered that. But as soon as he'd said it, she registered how ill-dressed she was in her nightshirt, dressing gown and slippers.

'No time to change though. And it gets cosy in there once you get moving.'

She swallowed hard; choked down the sourness of her fear. The aroma of earth was potent. She was ten again, crawling into her tiny cramped tent in the muddy campsite. Every one of her senses railed against what she was about to do. But, right now, she had no choice. Noah was in there, petrified and bound in the dark, and she had to reach him as quickly as she could by doing whatever she was asked. Until an opportunity presented itself.

'It curves left to a right angle. Don't rush. Haste is waste.'

Rose stepped up to the tunnel he'd indicated and shone the lantern around its interior. He was right. She could see about five feet inside and then the passage curved away. Although the ceiling was uneven, there was a wooden arch supporting it around three feet in. The side and floor looked compacted save for some small piles of mud that had fallen at intervals along its length. How deep under the ground would she be? At least the depth of the cellar staircase. What was that? Eight, ten feet? That was a lot of weight above. If it collapsed in on her, there would be no getting out.

She took a breath in, set the lantern just inside the rim and then gripped the bottom edge with her fingers. The soil was cold and friable. She released the fragments from her palms, got a better purchase and then hooked her right knee onto the edge. Rose nudged the lantern further inside and got her other knee up. Crouching down, she slid her top half into the passage and felt the cold of the tunnel floor seep through her chest as she lay flat.

As sound dampened, her breathing was suddenly very loud. She shoved the light ahead and extended her arms, pressing her elbows into the dirt and using her shoulders to haul herself forward.

Bloom said something behind Rose. It sounded close.

Her legs were still protruding from the opening, so she quickly pulled them in. Rose crawled further forward as quickly as she could. Now she was sure she was entirely inside.

She paused, closed her eyes. Felt her circulation pumping in her constricted body. No wonder Bloom needed her to get the case. His size would definitely be an issue in here. Perhaps that gave her an advantage. He wanted whatever was in here badly and she was his only way of getting it.

She struggled herself further up on her elbows and felt

the cold ceiling graze her scalp. It pressed harder when she filled her lungs. 'Noah!'

He answered and it sounded like he was behind the wall to her right.

'I'm coming! Don't be scared!' But her dried-out cry sounded so compressed.

A few fragments of dirt trickled into her hair.

Again, Noah yelled and he definitely sounded nearer. Could she dig through the wall to reach him?

'I'm here!' Her fingertips scratched at the surface beside her, but it was solid and she couldn't make an impression on it.

A low thudding sound.

That came from further ahead. Was it Noah? Rose gritted her teeth, pushed the lantern forward and squirmed after it.

Chapter Twenty-Six

Rose managed to get another seven feet along in the tunnel and then halted to listen again. The thudding had stopped and now all she could hear was the solid beat of her blood in the back of her head. She twisted her neck and looked along the length of her body to the ground she'd covered and couldn't see the mouth of the tunnel. She'd followed the gradual curve and it was now out of sight.

The thumping came again.

Actually, it sounded like it was a foot back from where she was. She reversed the distance and put her hand on the wall. She could feel the faint vibrations. How much earth was there between her and Noah?

Rose waited for the noise to stop and then beat the wall with her fist. 'I'm here!'

There was a pause and then she could hear his voice.

Much louder but she still couldn't make out what he was saying.

Again, she banged the wall. 'Can you hear me?' Her hand throbbed as she waited.

The hysteria in his response rose.

'Stay calm! I'm coming!' She clawed at the wall, but only thin slivers gave way under her nails.

'You can't burrow your way through there.' Bloom's voice sounded like he was at her shoulder.

She quickly turned. Was he crawling into the tunnel with her? Rose couldn't see any sign of movement. She grabbed the lantern and shone it behind her.

No trace of him.

'Four suitcases,' he reminded her. 'And you're inside the shortest tunnel.'

She slipped the lantern back and tried to use the plastic casing to chip away at the wall.

Noah was yelling at her again.

Larger fragments came away but when she paused to shine the light there, she could see the solid wet reddish-brown clay that had been exposed.

'I'm not a betting man, but if I was, I'd put money on your son's air supply running out first. Panic gobbles oxygen.'

He was right. Her own atmosphere was starting to taste stale and if Noah was gagged and already struggling because of his condition, she couldn't risk overexciting him. 'Noah, listen to me!'

He was babbling now.

'Noah. Stop talking. Please! Stop talking.'

She waited. Could just hear him weeping. She felt currents of helplessness and hatred for Bloom collide. 'Listen to me. Just concentrate on breathing. Breathe slowly. Like Doctor Sheldon showed you. Remember?'

Silence.

Was he doing it? 'Don't struggle anymore. Only answer when I call you. Can you hear me?'

Still nothing.

'Noah, just knock twice to tell me you heard me.' She puffed a damp strand of hair out of her eyes. Her forehead was already clammy.

A few moments later, two light bumps came.

She felt a droplet of relief. 'I'm right here and I'm coming to get you, but I have to do something else first. Keep doing your breathing exercises and don't shout any more. I'll be with you soon. I promise. Knock twice to tell me you understand.'

They came seconds after.

Rose exhaled and briefly rested her face on the cold floor of the tunnel. Bloom was right. She had to bring him the suitcases as fast as she could, otherwise Noah would be fighting for breath more than he already was. She shone the lantern ahead.

The tunnel curved away to the left so she could only see about six feet in front of her. How much further did she have to go?

The lantern flickered so she rapped her knuckles against the side. The light came back on.

She didn't want to lose her proximity to Noah but dragged herself forward, grunting her way into the thinner portion of the tunnel. Rose assumed this was the right angle that Bloom had mentioned.

She gripped its edge, swung herself around it and directed the lantern into the alcove. The silvery light picked out the dirt-covered shape of a black Samsonite suitcase.

Chapter Twenty-Seven

Cold prickled in the middle of Rose's shoulders. Whatever was inside the case was extremely valuable to Bloom. White, soil-covered and hairy roots had grown over it and hung about it like a weird lampshade. She negotiated her way through, but the passage was much narrower here, and she felt the ceiling and walls hug her body. She pushed the lantern forward and followed it, straining as she fought to round the bend with her entire body.

She reached out to the case but was still an inch or two away so waggled herself nearer until she could touch the bottom of it. The handle was visible on the right-hand side, so she slipped her fingers around and used the edge to pull herself tighter to it, her breath suddenly hot on her face.

'Do you see it yet?' Bloom's voice sounded so far away now.

'Yes. I've got it.' Hers sounded deafening.

'Quickly then,' he encouraged.

Rose's dirty fingers ran over the freezing handle and gave it a tug.

It wouldn't budge.

She tried again but it seemed to be lodged against the back of the tunnel. She managed to get her shoulder against the front edge and got a better purchase on the handle but when she jerked her body back hard, it still wouldn't move. She paused, breathing in her acrid air. 'Noah!'

A muted response.

'I'm still here! Try to breathe slowly!'

She couldn't understand his reply. The circulation in her restricted body pummelled her whole frame as she tried to discern what he was saying. 'I won't be long. Just sit tight!'

She clenched her body in readiness and then concentrated all her energy in her hand and wrist. She filled her chest and felt the tunnel tighten around her as she did.

She yanked on the handle and it scraped a few inches from its resting place. As it did, soil poured in on her.

Panic accelerated her heart rate as she waited for the disturbance to subside but she felt its cold weight on the back of her head and had to hold her face to the floor so she could maintain a pocket of air.

The earth kept hissing and trickling over her hair. She held her breath and waited.

A few moments later it stopped, started again and then stopped.

Rose lifted her mouth clear of the floor and blew fine soil from her lips. From what she could feel, it appeared to have covered her shoulders and the top of her head. She shook it and the dirt was flicked away from her hair. Spitting it out, she gripped the handle again. But if she tried to loosen it anymore, would the ceiling cave in?

She swallowed, tried to calm herself. Her mouth was already dehydrated. She wondered if more of the ceiling had collapsed behind her, cutting off her exit and her air. But when she rocked her body from side to side, she felt the mud rolling off her. Hopefully, it was mainly coming off the roots and not the ceiling above.

There was only one thing for it – forget easing it out, she would drag the case as quickly as she could from the recess and retreat around the bend to the main tunnel. If the alcove crumbled, she should be safer back where Noah was and there was more room to move.

Rose put her other hand over the front edge of the case and gripped the handle firmly. Gritting her teeth, she heaved on it firmly, using the muscles in her shoulders to pull it out.

It jolted out a few more inches and she could hear roots tearing as soil rained down from above.

'Come on!'

She pumped her body in the confined space, her stomach going taut as the case stubbornly stayed in place. She dug her toes into the dirt and her body went rigid as she wrenched back.

More roots ripping and soil cascading in on her.

'Move!'

Her shriek freed the right corner of the case and she slid back a few inches as it came away. She cried out again, spittle on her lips as its bulk came towards her.

Rose could feel that it was almost clear and tugged it repeatedly until it shifted another foot from the roots. Her tendons felt like they were being stretched to their limits, but she maintained the tension until it came free.

As it did, the ceiling above her opened and the weight of the earth landed heavily on top of her.

Chapter Twenty-Eight

Rose spat grit as she snaked her way backwards from the alcove. She still had hold of the case but the weight of the debris from above made it too heavy to drag with her. Crawling forward a few inches, she swept dirt off the lid, seized the handle with both hands and lugged it towards her. Four short and sharp tugs got it moving again and she felt the muscles in her shoulders trembling like they would tear as she put her face down. She could feel her heels against the right angle of the tunnel wall and used them to brace herself before pulling as hard as her body would allow.

The case slid from the recess, and she immediately raised her head and sucked in air before lifting her hands from the mounds of soil covering them. There was no light. Where was the lantern? Rose scrabbled in the dried mud for it and her fingers clasped the casing. The space was illuminated again. She dropped the light over her shoulder, slid her legs back down the main tunnel and turned her torso to follow so she could heave the case completely clear of the alcove.

Grabbing the lantern from beside her, Rose examined the mildewed suitcase. Would it be as weighty now that it was clear of its resting place? She used the handle to hiss it half a foot after her. It was heavy but moved easier. 'Noah!'

No answer.

'Noah!' She turned her head back down the tunnel.

A response but muted.

Taking the lantern with her, she wormed her way backwards to the spot where his voice had been loudest. 'You have to answer me every time!' She put her ear to the cool wall.

'I did.'

Rose understood that. 'You OK?'

He replied but it was garbled, sentences running into each other. She waited for him to finish. 'Just breathe. Only talk when I call and just say OK, OK?'

'OK.'

Exhaling, she shone the lantern back to the case.

'Progress?' Bloom's word reverberated around her.

'Yes.' But a new thought had occurred to her. 'I've got it. Black case,' she confirmed. Rose bit her lip as she played the light over the piece of luggage.

'Are you stuck?'

'No.' She turned her head back to where he was. He couldn't see her because she was concealed by the curve. She scrabbled back to the case and placed her palms on it. Now that she had a little more space, could she turn it? She did and was soon looking at the combination catches.

'I hope you're not getting too comfortable in there.'

Her caked fingers shook at the first catch but when she pressed down, it was solid. Locked.

'There's another two tunnels for you to explore yet.'

Rose grunted as she tried the second. Locked too.

'Not sure Noah's got time to kill.'

If he'd gone to all this trouble to get the case, then surely she had leverage while it was still in her possession.

'Rose?'

'Let him go first.'

A pause.

'You're going back on our deal already?' There wasn't a trace of levity in his voice now.

Rose shivered as his flat response vibrated around her. 'Let him out of there. I want to hear his voice from where you are. Then I'll bring the case out.'

No words echoed back, only an almost imperceptible sigh.

'We'll get the cases for you. Together. Noah and I. That's the only way we're doing this.'

Rose was already thinking ahead. She could renegotiate when they got to the last case.

Get Noah out of harm's way before Bloom got what he wanted.

'No, Rose. Make me wait a second longer and I'm going to use the bread knife you gave me to saw your son's throat open.'

Chapter Twenty-Nine

R ose heard movement at the end of the tunnel and shone the lantern in its direction. Scrabbling and heavy breathing. The faint light from the cellar was suddenly blocked. 'Wait!'

But the disturbance continued, and it seemed as if Bloom were panting in her ear. Rose anticipated his face appearing around the curve before her. But he'd said this tunnel was the tightest one. Could he even fit in here now?

The noise stopped. Silence.

'I'm bringing it now!' She waited for his answer. Then realisation clutched her chest. 'Noah?' Had Bloom just entered the tunnel where her son was?

No reply.

'I'm bringing it out! I'm bringing it out now!' Rose seized the handle in both hands and started shuddering it out of the tunnel. But when it slid to the right, it got lodged there. 'Then I'll get the next one. Like we agreed!'

She shot a look behind her again, but Bloom wasn't there.

Rose had to shove the case back up the tunnel to loosen it, but it was stuck fast. She hammered it with the heel of her hands, but it wouldn't budge. 'I'm nearly there! I'm nearly out!'

But the next sound was Noah's scream.

Rose's ear was back to the earth wall. 'Noah! Answer me!' She could hear her son's voice, indiscernible again. He was babbling. No. Pleading. Pleading with her... or Bloom? Was he with her son now? 'Noah!'

Get out of the tunnel now. Find Noah.

She grabbed the lantern and frantically reversed away from the lodged case.

Save Noah. Use the lantern as a weapon.

She yelled as she tried to backtrack faster but wriggled into the curve and started pushing herself up the wall. As raw panic took hold, she had to turn to navigate.

Her son's voice was receding. She couldn't hear him any longer. 'Noah!'

Find them. Cave Bloom's brains in.

She peered back, could see light spilling around the corner from the cellar again. Bloom was definitely not in her tunnel. Only another ten feet and she would be clear.

But Rose halted, her fingers dug into the floor.

There was no way she could take Bloom by surprise.

Her body quaked as she fought every instinct to get out and defend Noah. The light in her hand illuminated the case.

She hastily crawled back towards it. 'I've got the case! I've got it! I'm coming out!'

Rose shouted the words repeatedly as she reached it and waggled it from side to side where it was trapped. 'If you want the others, you'd better not touch him! Answer me!'

Her exclamation boosted her strength and the case shot back at her. The lantern rolled off to the side and the light went out. Rose didn't wait though. She dragged the case back and put her ear to the wall again.

No sound from the other side.

'Noah!'

No movement. Nothing.

'I've got it!' She didn't feel any pain as she ground her body back along the grit in the floor to the entrance of the cellar.

Rose was back in the anteroom, her slippered feet on the ground. As she got upright, she didn't turn but hefted the case from the entrance of the tunnel before swivelling with it into the dazzling light of the cellar.

Chapter Thirty

S he squinted against the intense glow of the room as the weight of the case bent her forward. She released the handle, and the case dropped and thudded at her feet. She put the edge of her hand across her eyebrows. Was Bloom in the cellar? There were no dark blobs within the brightness of the white painted brick walls. Rose reminded herself that he still had her bread knife.

She blinked rapidly until the room emerged from the glare. No sign of him. She turned back to the anteroom. Was he still in the tunnel with Noah? There was no sound of anyone coming out. Her body pulsed as she waited.

Thud.

That came from above her head. He was back upstairs. Had he taken Noah there too? She ran to the foot of the staircase but the door above rattled, and she retreated again.

Rose's eyes flitted about the empty cellar. Where could she hide?

The door opened slowly and more artificial light from above crawled down the stairs.

The case. She had to shift it from sight. Padding back to the hole, she used all her strength to lift and carry it silently over to the clear area under the stairs.

A creak above her.

Bloom was walking stealthily down them. Should she stay there?

But he didn't descend any further. His feet shuffled on the spot.

Rose heard the door close, and the key being turned in the lock. Now she was trapped. *Think.* How long would it take him to find her? Even if he went into the tunnels hunting for her, he still had the key and she couldn't get out of the cellar. It was only a matter of time before he discovered her.

Silence from above.

She briefly closed her eyes and knew she had to misdirect him from where she'd hidden the case.

The next stair creaked as he put his weight onto it. She looked up, could see the outline of his ankle on it.

Go now. Rose took a breath but couldn't bring herself to move. *Go now!*

The third stair squeaked.

Rose braced herself and then slipped out from under the stairs and stole back towards the anteroom.

Another cautious footstep on the staircase.

Then she clocked the three darts in the board. She dashed over to it and pulled all three out. Wait. He'd notice they were all gone. She'd put two back. Where the hell had they been? She remembered one had been in the triple twenty, replaced it and stuck the other near it. The third she put in the pocket of her dressing gown.

The footfalls accelerated.

Rose darted back to the anteroom, reversed into the shadows but faced the cellar. She waited for him to appear at the bottom of the stairs, her breath coming in short bursts.

Bloom reached the cellar floor as his attention immediately focused on where she was standing. Could he see her? He pocketed the key.

His right pocket. Remember.

He cocked his head to one side as he peered into the shadows.

He couldn't see her. But Rose realised she had to sell him the idea that she hadn't been in the cellar. She leaned back against the tunnel she'd emerged from and wriggled herself against its edge to make some noise.

Bloom remained where he was.

She watched his body relax and a small smile play about his mouth. Where was the bread knife?

She put her hand back in the pocket of her dressing gown to double-check the dart was still there. She felt it prick her fingertip. It was a tiny weapon but one he didn't know she had. Would he notice it missing? She had to get close enough to him to use it before he did.

'Rose?' He was looking straight at her.

How well could he see her? She made a little more noise, grunted and then staggered out of the shadows.

The smile on his lips evaporated.

Rose held a hand to her eyes as she had the first time she'd exited the tunnel. 'Where's Noah?'

Bloom looked up at the ceiling. 'Safe upstairs. Where's the case?'

Chapter Thirty-One

'Tell me exactly where he is.'

Bloom's gaze was still upward. 'Listen.'

But there was nothing.

'Noah, answer me!' Rose yelled.

A thumping sound from above.

Bloom's eyes met hers. 'He's in a less stressful environment now. He's got plenty of air and light, but I had to make sure he wouldn't run.'

She felt anger and dread balloon. 'What have you done to him?'

'Made sure he wouldn't run,' he enunciated gently. The affability returned to his expression.

But Rose recalled what he'd threatened to do to her son only moments earlier.

'So, I realise that, given the long list of things I asked

you to bring out of the tunnel, one of them may have slipped your mind…'

Rose dropped her hand from her eyes but still squinted at him.

'Just that one thing that has a significant bearing on the situation upstairs.'

'It's just back there.' She jerked her thumb behind her.

'"Just back there." Not in here?' He fixated on an empty spot on the concrete floor in front of her.

'It was heavy. I had to make sure Noah was safe.'

'Understandable. But you know he is now.' He didn't look up from the floor.

Had he heard her in the cellar before he'd come down the stairs? 'I couldn't drag it any further. It got jammed.'

He raised his pure blue eyes to her. 'So, I'm going to have to do it myself? Forget our deal?'

She shook her head emphatically. 'I'll go back. I can try to loosen it. But it was stuck fast.' She had to get Bloom closer. Make him walk past the dartboard so it was no longer in his eyeline.

But Bloom stayed where he was. 'Do that. Do that and I promise you can walk up those stairs and check on Noah.' His eyes remained on hers.

'OK.' She couldn't afford to hesitate and reveal she knew he'd locked the door. Was he playing with her?

Bloom raised a wiry eyebrow.

'It's just inside the entrance here. I'll do what I can.'

138

He still didn't budge. All it was going to take was a look left and he'd know she had the dart.

Rose turned, crawled back in the tunnel and rotated herself in the cramped space so she could look back at him.

He'd walked a few more paces towards the anteroom but had stopped dead opposite the dartboard.

Rose thumped the wall a few times and grunted.

Bloom advanced. He was past the dartboard.

Now he didn't know she had a weapon. Didn't know the case was sitting behind him.

'Are you going to make a career of this, Rose? There are three more cases to find yet.' He was nearly at the anteroom.

Rose took the dart out of her pocket and gripped the point hard between her forefinger and thumb. He couldn't see her in the darkness. If she could just get him to peer into the tunnel.

He hesitated. 'Where's the lantern, Rose?'

'I dropped it when I was crawling out.'

'Find it.'

'I'll have to pull this case out first before I can go back and get it.'

Bloom considered that for a few seconds.

Rose watched him scratch his earlobe, heard the clink of his signet ring against his ear jewellery. She gripped the dart point harder. She would have to aim for his eye.

Then he bent down and leaned into the tunnel.

Chapter Thirty-Two

R ose drew her clenched fist back, but a light dazzled
her.

'Better?'

She put her other hand to her eyes but couldn't conceal
the weapon at her side quick enough. The glare was coming
from a phone he was holding. Her phone.

'I can see my lantern back there. Grab it. You'll need it in
the other tunnels. Then you can drag the case out from
behind the stairs for me.'

Rose blinked against the light but didn't move. He must
have heard her before she crept back to the tunnel.

'If you're going to stick that dart in me, hurry up and do
it. Get it out of your system.'

Rose kept it clenched in her fist.

'You've still got a lot of work ahead of you, though, and

I'm sure Noah won't thank you for complicating matters.' He remained in position; light still held in her face. 'You don't want him tied up any longer than he needs to be, do you?'

Rose momentarily closed her eyes and felt the energy drain from her.

'It's not four feet from you. Just crawl over there and fetch it.'

She turned to where the beam illuminated the tunnel behind her. The lantern was lying where she'd discarded it.

Crawling on her hands and knees, she picked it up. Could she slug him with it when she turned?

As if reading her thoughts, Bloom reversed a few paces but kept the light of her phone trained on Rose. 'Come on out of there.' He extended an arm to steady her.

She ignored it and dropped her feet back onto the floor of the anteroom.

Bloom retreated with each step Rose took as she walked back into the cellar.

'Get the case for me.' He didn't turn to the stairs.

Rose took a pace forward, but he held up a hand.

'I'm a bit of a completist. Do you mind?' He nodded at the dartboard opposite.

Rose replaced the dart in the board. He still had her bread knife but there was no sign of it about his person. Was it in his back pocket?

'OK. Slide it there.' He pointed to an area on the floor.

Rose went over to the case and dragged it over on its narrowest side to where he'd indicated, the combination catches uppermost.

'I feel the need to impress on you the value of what you're doing for me.'

Rose gripped the lantern hard in her right hand, but he wasn't near enough for her to take a swing.

Bloom examined the case with interest. 'In pretty good shape, considering.'

'Let me go upstairs and check on Noah.'

His eyes remained on the case.

'If you don't let me, I won't go on with this.'

He looked up at her and there was amused pity in his expression. 'I'm a man of my word. But I'm going to need to see something better than the display of subterfuge we've had from you so far.'

'I promise I'll do whatever you want. Anything.' She let the significance of that hang between them.

Bloom's face remained impassive but slyness registered in his eyes.

'Just let me go up and see him... for a moment.'

'He's better off up there for now. We have something to do here first.'

Rose knew he wanted her to ask him to qualify the remark, but she waited.

'I'm going to open this up.' Bloom switched off and pocketed her phone and knelt in front of the case.

'I don't need to see what's inside.' She took a step backward.

Bloom nodded distractedly and started rolling the combination numbers.

Chapter Thirty-Three

'I gave you the lightest one to bring out first.' Bloom stuck out his tongue as he spun the last number wheel on the second catch. 'There.' He put his thumbs against them both and they thudded open.

She could feel them resonate in her chest, but Rose's attention shot to the stairs. Her eyes darted back to Bloom as he shifted his attention to her.

He blinked once and then allowed the case to fall open.

At first Rose thought she was looking at some clothes. Mint-green elastic belts crossed and secured them in both halves of the case. They were inside shrivelled vacuum-packed plastic and they looked yellowed by age.

'Meet Pamela Grant. Pam, Rose. Rose, Pam.' Bloom remained crouching by the case, no trace of humour on his face as he made the introductions.

She was looking at jaundiced, aged skin. Rose's hand

shot to her mouth as she identified an arm curled inside one of the packages. The fingers of the hand were clenched into a fist, the nails long and black. A hissing started in Rose's ear as repulsion swept over her.

'Pam's my oldest house guest. And yours.'

Her eyes reluctantly scanned the rest of the contents of the case before she could close them. They registered the sole of a foot in the other compartment.

'She had anorexia. Weighed very little. Three weeks off her nineteenth birthday.'

Rose swayed, nausea melting her kneecaps. She opened her eyes again as she tottered back a pace.

'Second year of college. Modern history. Just broken up for the summer break. She was a popular girl loved by students and teachers alike. But then they always say that, don't they? I've yet to see someone being interviewed about a missing or dead girl who says she'll be no great loss.' He stood and cocked his head at Rose, as if waiting for a reaction.

Rose was thinking about how close she'd come to using the dart. If he was capable of this, what chance would she have stood? And what chance did she have of saving Noah? Her head began to tremble.

'I want you to understand why Pam's so precious to me. Why all of our house guests are.' He brushed his palms lightly against each other.

'Please... I'm begging you.' But she already knew that was pointless. 'I won't tell anyone about this,' she heard herself say. The words sounded bassy, like she was talking underwater. But she stopped, knew what his patient expression meant.

'Our secret, eh? Could you really live with something like this?'

Rose nodded categorically. But it was obvious whatever he said was lies. A performance to make sure she did what he asked. And he didn't care that she knew it. He couldn't let them go. That's why he'd opened the case. If she was terrified of him, he could be sure of her cooperation for however long he needed her alive.

'She was the youngest. Thought she was in her early twenties when I walked past her on the green. It's difficult to tell at that age though. They all want to look older. I didn't know I'd abducted a teenager until I caught it on the news.'

Now Rose couldn't move. Couldn't summon the energy she needed to stir her legs. But where could she go? Back into the tunnels? Try to find a way up to the lawn? But Noah was upstairs. With her son tied up, Bloom could be sure of her obedience.

'She had a tattoo on her wrist. A Celtic symbol. Do you have any tattoos?'

Rose shook her head.

'I've never been tempted. Haven't ever got past the idea that you're having something inked on you that will allow the police to ID you.' He tilted his eyes to the case. 'Glad to see the vacuum bags holding out. They look a little brittle now. Doesn't bear thinking about what would happen if you pierced one of those. I kept Pam in the attic for the best part of five months. That's why I came up with the idea of sealing her up after I dismembered her.'

Rose just looked at the shaved crown of his head – she couldn't bring herself to look into the case again. Her throat pumped once but nothing came up. The sick weight of her predicament and what it meant for Noah expanded in her stomach.

'I was getting the Christmas decorations up from down here when I found the stud wall. There were stacks of empty gin bottles behind it. One of the previous owners must have sneaked down here to drink in private. I started digging it out on New Year's Day. Seemed like a good time to start. Lost a couple of days but I still hadn't finished when I had to start back to work.'

Rose only met his eye when she realised he'd stopped talking.

'You OK there, Rose?'

Chapter Thirty-Four

'I didn't know Pam until she briefly glanced at me as she walked by me on Feltham Green with her King Charles spaniel. It was the usual way young girls regarded me. Not with any degree of distaste but one hundred per cent indifference. That's never particularly bothered me. I've always thought of being invisible as a virtue. It means I can be present, observe and absorb without being acknowledged. Being a removal man allows me that. To access people's lives and rarely be noticed.'

Rose took a faltering step back from the case and felt the wall against her back.

'I'm the kid that skulked at the back of school class photos and made sure the head of the child in front was obscuring me. It infuriated my mother.'

Her only chance of escape was to knock him out cold and get the key from his pocket but even though he was crouching before her, there was too much space between them to take him by surprise.

'Pam went on her way and so did I. Opposite directions. But her perfume settled on me as she passed by. It was a little like the dewberry scent my girlfriend, Laura, used to wear. I hadn't thought about her in a long while. I wondered where she was right then. Probably married and doing something with her family. That could have been me, but I was glad it wasn't. The whole three and a half years we'd been an item, I couldn't shake the notion we were both just going through some preconceived motions, ticking the boxes until we crossed the Rubicon. I saw marriage looming. My ultimate fear. Not the commitment but the inevitable fixing of a date to be in the spotlight. That's when I pulled the plug.'

It was more terrifying than bizarre that Bloom was suddenly opening up to her in this way. Was he doing so because he knew she would never utter a word of what he said?

'Pam's perfume faded as I walked on. Having spent those years with Laura, I'd really expected to miss her, but I didn't. Her presence evaporated just as quickly.'

Run to the top of the stairs. Even if the door was locked, she could try to push him down them when he chased her up there. But Rose figured he wouldn't panic. As long as he had the key, he knew she wasn't going anywhere.

'Thinking about Laura, I'd forgotten about Pam by the time I'd reached the main gates and crossed the gravel of the small parking area. My white Renault was the only vehicle left. It was still sunny but the handful of people who had come to walk or bring a picnic had headed home. I wouldn't normally have been out at that time on a Monday afternoon but the batteries in my smoke detector had needed replacing. I'd parked up behind the green to avoid having to pay in town, and cut through to the hardware store. It was thinking about those batteries that made me stop dead. I checked my inside pocket...' Bloom mimed the action as if it were aiding his memory. 'The new packet of batteries was in there, but I'd forgotten to pick up the one good one left I'd taken in with me, so I knew which number it was. Stupid mistake.'

Rose's eyes were on his right pocket that contained the key.

He sighed and checked his watch, reliving the episode. 'Ten to five. If I hurried, I'd catch the hardware shop before it closed. It was all down to that decision, Rose. I could have just gone home then. Or maybe it was because of what happened a few moments later. Hard to tell.'

Rose met his eye.

'I walked back through the gates and to the green. A hundred yards later, I saw Pam again, walking back towards me with her King Charles on a lead. As she approached, I decided to make eye contact. We'd literally just passed each other and here we were about to do it again. Had she also forgotten something, or had she simply walked the dog to the edge of the green and back again?

Regardless, if I hadn't felt flustered about the battery and trying to catch the shop before it closed, I maybe would have kept my eyes on the dirt path.'

Rose again considered the tunnel Noah had been held in. Could she get out to the lawn that way? But the whole section had collapsed. She might end up trapped and trying to dig her way out while Bloom had plenty of time to make his way upstairs.

'When her eyes met mine, she gave me the same look. There wasn't even a hint of recognition. Perhaps that *was* the moment. Pam didn't know it though. She passed by again, yanking her dog when it tried to sniff me, as if she thought I might be contagious. I just continued on my way but after ten or twelve paces, I halted. Something I'd always wondered occurred to me then and I turned on my heel.'

Rose's frantic thoughts briefly halted.

'Pam only half looked over her shoulder when I was a pace behind her. When I saw the earbuds, I realised she was listening to her music. When my fist struck the back of her head, one of them popped out.'

Rose's breath caught.

'Pam didn't make a sound as she hit the ground. She was dazed and seemed confused as to what to do first: keep hold of the animal or fend off her attacker. She opted for the former, so I slammed my fist into her face. She looked up as it connected, and I caught her full force in the forehead. Coldcocked her. Her body was laid out flat, both her hands on her chest. Out for the count.' He looked into the open case as if seeing her remains would jog the recollection.

The cellar was briefly silent as they both visualised the moment.

'My fist was buzzing and the dog barked at me. Only a few times though. It scuttled a few feet away and looked over its shoulder at me. Like she had. Then Pam released its lead and it ran away further. I looked up and down the path. Nobody coming in either direction and the dog just kept circling me. There was a wooded area to my right. The parking area was just beyond that. I knew I could easily drag her through that way and put her in the back of my Renault. I was confident I wouldn't be seen. I was never seen. But if someone did accost me, I could just say I'd found her and was taking her to the hospital. That made up my mind. I'd drag her in there. Leave her in the foliage. Then I promised myself that if she was still there after I'd picked up my battery from the hardware store, I'd put her in my car.'

Chapter Thirty-Five

'I t was the most spur-of-the-moment thing I've ever done.'

Rose was looking at Bloom's hands. He was still gently wiping his palms against each other. His description of Pam's abduction sounded almost sentimental.

'Being impulsive was something my ex said I was incapable of.'

Rose felt sickened by his account. And if he'd inflicted such casual violence on a random teenage girl, there was no chance that he would exhibit any mercy towards her and Noah.

'She was of such slight build. I wasn't quite the weight I am now, but I knew I could easily overpower her. I was also sure she'd be there when I returned. She never woke up. I drove around for a couple of hours with her on the floor in the back, just in case she came to. Just doing circles of the neighbourhood. Stupid really. I stopped when I realised how suspicious that would look on the street cameras. And I was sure she wouldn't open her eyes.'

'Noah!' Rose yelled and she heard him weakly shout back through his gag from upstairs.

It didn't appear to puncture Bloom's reverie. 'I made a lot of errors. But I didn't really know I was abducting her until I drove home. I dropped one of my contact lenses.' He looked up from the case at Rose as if expecting a reaction.

Her face remained frozen. She didn't blink.

'Didn't notice until I got home. I panicked and went back to the green a few hours later. Had to Google for any cases of DNA being sampled from them. There was, so I had to scour the area. Another stupid mistake but this time I went back on foot and entered by a different gate. Never found it. I've stuck to spectacles ever since. Always leave them in the van now.'

Noah yelled for Rose again.

'Let me go to him,' she whispered.

Bloom frowned. 'I'd always wondered if I was truly invisible to everyone. Pam Grant taught me I was. I took her so casually, so effortlessly. It was a steep learning curve for me. I'd only just got used to wearing contacts.' His eyes smiled at his own joke.

Rose felt sickened to be a part of his reminiscence. She took a faltering breath in and could smell the mould of the case.

'There was nothing on the news about her for three

days. Even though other people would have seen her walking her dog on the green. I was gobsmacked. Got tired of waiting to be arrested. By the time her parents were on TV asking for her safe return, I'd suffocated her with a pillow.' He surveyed the interior of the case.

Rose didn't follow his gaze.

'I still feel guilty about the dog.'

She was watching his mouth move, and it seemed as if it was slightly out of sync with what he was saying.

'I looked for it when I went back for my contact lens. It had been circling her in the foliage when I carried her to the car. From a distance. There was no sign of it in the evening. Must have just wandered off.'

Bloom gently closed the case and fixed the catches.

Both felt like bullets to Rose's chest.

'I was genuinely shocked by how quickly Pam became old news. Struggled to find any sort of info on the case only a few weeks later. She became as invisible as me. When it was safe, I went to her family home in the early hours of the morning. It was barely ten minutes from here. I had her in my car, and I was going to dump her on their doorstep. At least let them bury her. Give them closure. But, at the last minute, I decided against it. I told myself that it was because I didn't want to remove their last hope. That part of them could believe she was still alive somewhere. But I also didn't want to get caught. And when I asked myself why I didn't, I already had the answer.'

So did Rose.

'There was only one other like Pam. One occasion that was entirely unpremeditated.' His eyes darted to the stairs and back to meet Rose's. Then he stood, put his hand in his right pocket and pulled out the key. 'Full disclosure, the door to upstairs is locked. You'll need this if you want to get to Noah and so will I.' He threw it.

It landed with a metallic clunk at her feet.

'Pick it up. It's yours.'

Chapter Thirty-Six

R ose didn't look down at it.

'Or would you rather a cash prize?'

Would he attack her when she bent to pick it up? After the story he'd told her, perhaps he was sure she wouldn't try anything. She still couldn't see the bread knife about him.

'OK, answer the following question: would you like to see Noah again? Yes or no?'

She nodded.

'Yes or no?'

'Yes!'

'Pick up the key then.'

Without taking her eyes from Bloom, she bent to her knees and felt about on the concrete. The metal was cold on her hot palm, and she scooped it up and quickly stood.

Bloom remained where he was. 'OK, now only you can

open the door to upstairs.'

Rose gripped it hard in her hand. He could take it back off her any time he wanted. She was defenceless against his brawn. If he'd murdered Pam Grant with such spontaneous brutality…

'It's a gesture of trust. You go back in there for me'—he nodded towards the tunnels—'and you know Noah will be safe while you are.'

Rose felt a tiny pang of relief. It was clear he still needed her.

'I won't be able to access upstairs while you're inside the tunnel and you have the key in your pocket.'

That was correct. All the keys for the doors were different. There was only one for the cellar door. But how long would she be useful to him? Were there really that many cases for her to pull out or would the next one be the last? He could then overpower her to get the key.

'It's your insurance.'

'And you think I trust you to let us go after what you've just told me?' Rose's left leg trembled violently.

'I told you that so you understand who I am and why the cases are so valuable to me.' Bloom briefly looked down at her leg and raised his hands. 'I've already said I need to get everything loaded up outside afterwards. Outside, Rose. We can negotiate another insurance when we're at that stage but, at the moment, we're far from it. And we're wasting time.'

Rose shook her head.

'You're saying no. The person with no choice is saying no?' He took a step forward.

Rose retreated and her shoulders bumped against the wall behind her again.

He held out his palms to placate her. 'You can move faster than me and the sooner I have my luggage in an alternative location, the sooner I can have peace of mind.'

Rose braced herself against the bricks. 'Let me go up there right now.'

Bloom sighed, his shoulders lifting and falling. 'This is a gesture. And one you don't deserve. Next case first. Or you lose the key. If you're no good to me down here, I'll guarantee you'll be no good to Noah up there.' The threat was explicit. He raised his wiry dark eyebrows.

If she refused, she was dead. If she agreed, the outcome was likely to be the same, but she would temporarily keep Noah out of danger and buy herself a little more time.

'Want me to take it back?' He didn't move any closer.

But he didn't need to. Rose shook her head.

'Good. Time to clock back in.'

'Which one now then?' Rose unstuck her sweating back from the wall.

'Tunnel one, my first excavation. It's not quite as tight as the last.'

Rose felt her shoulders prickle. 'It couldn't possibly be.' There had barely been enough air in that one.

'I need you to take care though. Handle this case delicately. They're a good friend of mine.'

Chapter Thirty-Seven

Rose put the key into her dressing gown pocket. 'I bring this next case out and I want to see Noah.'

Bloom angled his blank expression at her.

'I go up there to check on him.'

He nodded slightly. 'OK.'

Rose waited for a 'but'.

Bloom gestured towards the anteroom.

'Agreed?'

'I've just said OK.'

She turned uncertainly towards the tunnels and then swivelled back to him.

He hadn't moved. 'Wiggle, wiggle, little worm.'

Rose tried the switch of the lantern a few times and tapped it so it came on. It illuminated her muddy nightclothes. She swung it behind her and stood before the anteroom. Before her was the tunnel where he'd kept Noah.

If she got into that one, was there even a small chance she could dig up to the lawn as he had? If she could, he would have to follow her. He couldn't get out of the cellar if she had the key. Could she release Noah and get clear of the house before he crawled up after her? She kept the light off its entrance.

'The one to your far left.'

She immediately shifted the lantern over to it. He had to know what was running through her head.

'It's still a squeeze but you should be able to move faster.'

He was right. The entrance to the tunnel was a little larger than the first one.

'My younger self had no problem. And I would have still been a good few pounds heavier than you.'

Rose inhaled a few times and then placed the lantern on the floor of the tunnel. The light shone all the way along it. No gentle curve, only blackness at the end.

Sliding herself into the passage, she dug her fingers into the cold floor and pulled herself all the way inside. As soon as she did, however, a horrible thought occurred to her. Had he really given her the key to the cellar door?

Rose pushed her hand behind her into her gown pocket and brought it up to her face. She shone the light on it. It looked like the key. But every door in the house had one like it. All of them slightly different. Was it the right one? There was no way of telling.

She stopped breathing; tried to listen for the sound of

Bloom climbing the stairs, but her body was blocking the tunnel so she couldn't discern the activity in the cellar. What could he do in the time she was in the tunnel? Was that why he'd agreed to let her see Noah after she'd got the case? With her out of the way, he could do what he wanted. Why would he offer to lock himself in the cellar when he didn't need to?

Rose remained stiff inside the mouth of the tunnel. 'Can you hear me back there?'

'Loud and clear,' he eventually replied.

His voice sounded so distant to Rose. Was he now standing at the top of the stairs?

Thunk.

What was that sound?

Thunk, thunk.

It was the darts thudding into the board again.

'I'm losing my touch.'

At least she knew he was still in the cellar. Rose weighed up non-existent options. If he had deceived her and wanted to go upstairs, it was unlikely she could stop him.

Get the case. Bring it out. He promised to let me see Noah then.

Rose pocketed the key and inched forward, fibrous roots above dragging over the top of her head. But as she made slow progress, the tunnel hugged her tighter and she realised her body was sloping down. The shaft was getting thinner and it looked like she was going deeper underground.

Chapter Thirty-Eight

Eight feet later, Rose felt her body conforming to gravity. When she lifted her elbows, she began to slide downward. Her heart thumped in her ears, it got even colder, and the smell of clay became potent. What if she dropped all the way down and got stuck? Would she even be able to turn around and clamber back up?

She halted by digging in her hands, but her arms trembled as she fought to stop herself from slipping further. Bloom had been down here. And he must have been bigger than her, even when he was pounds lighter. Her breath misted about her face.

Releasing her hold, she allowed herself to glide down to the bottom and struck it hard, winding herself and bruising her ribs. She released a groan but closed her mouth against it. She didn't want to hear herself and nobody else could.

She let her circulation slow a little and then lifted the lantern and shone it ahead.

It illuminated a blank wall of red clay. No case.

Was this a trick? Was there only one case Bloom wanted and now he'd got her to crawl into her grave so he could seal it up? He could be filling in the hole right now. Then what would he do to Noah?

Her body went rigid, but she told herself she couldn't afford to lose it. She lifted the lantern and realised, with relief, that she was at the bottom of a V. The passage continued upwards. She snaked herself forwards and then gripped the clay. It was solid and freezing. She hauled herself up.

At eye level was another alcove and the light caught the familiar black object lodged there. Rose tried not to think about who was inside and how long ago they'd been unceremoniously deposited here.

She positioned the lantern in front of the case and then reached over to pull it out, but it was stuck fast. No roots had grown around it here. Why wouldn't it budge?

Rose tried again, felt the muscles in her arms and shoulders complain and her bruised stomach ache underneath her. She took hold of the handle with both hands again, gripped it tight and heaved but it didn't shift an inch. Her breath clouded before her, and her blood raced as she prepared for another go.

But there was so little room to move she could only use

the strength of her arms to try and dislodge it. Another two attempts left her breathless. Her oxygen supply had to be running out. What would happen if she couldn't bring the case up? If she could get out at all? She could feel the icy floor numbing her stomach. Maybe the case was frozen to the wall.

She had an idea. Reaching under her, she untied the dressing gown belt around her waist and, by shifting the weight off her stomach, managed to pull it clear of the two loops it was secured by and tugged it up to her face.

Rose wound a third of the belt around the handle and knotted it there. She wrapped the other end around her knuckles and yanked hard on the belt. No movement. Trying again, she tried to jerk it repeatedly, but she was too restricted by the low ceiling of the passage.

'Come on,' she growled.

The belt squeaked as it tightened with each sharp pull. Was it going to snap?

She needed more room to heave it out. Reversing herself back down to the bottom of the V, Rose used her entire weight on the belt, maintained the tension and curled herself against it as she heard the stitching start to break. Her wrists shook and the belt sliced into her fingers, but she thought she heard some movement above her. Was the case unsticking?

A ripping sound but she kept all her weight taut even as the belt stretched, and she slid further down. Her shoulders shook and her stomach muscles tremored. The belt had cut off the blood supply to her fingers, but she used her other hand to wrench it harder.

Something was about to give, and she was sure it would be the belt. Her temples pounded as she screwed her eyes shut and released a guttural cry.

A sliding noise from above and then she was struck hard on the head by the weight of the case. The impact slammed her teeth shut.

Don't black out.

Warm orange bubbles oozed over her brain.

Chapter Thirty-Nine

R ose got both her hands under the case's weight, but it appeared to be lodged there. She unstuck her sweating scalp from its underside and shifted her head cautiously down. It didn't drop any further. She opened her eyes, but yellow clouds filled her vision. She retrieved the lantern from where it was lying and shone it above.

The case was resting in the aperture, belt hanging down from the handle and still connected to her fist. It looked like it could fall on her any minute, so she slid back a foot and then unwound the belt from her fingers. She had no sensation in them and massaged her numb digits until she could bend them again.

There was no time to waste but it felt like the tunnel was turning around her. She closed her eyes, waiting for the sensation to subside. It didn't and suddenly she was shivering. Her teeth chattered uncontrollably and nausea rushed in. Did she have concussion? Was she going into shock? She didn't have time for either.

Rose tried to blink the yellow blobs out of her eyes as she positioned the lantern on the floor so it was shining upwards and took hold of the belt.

One tug and the case upended and thudded onto the floor of the V.

She decided to leave the belt tied to the handle so she could use it to drag it as she reversed up the incline of the tunnel. But the case got stuck with the first pull. Rose would have to reposition it each time she hauled it. She had the case now though and when she got back to the cellar, Bloom had promised she could see Noah. She used that thought to block out everything else.

Move backwards. Drag the case. Reposition it. Move again.

How far had she slid down the incline? It felt like she should be level again by now, but her body was still angled downward, which made the case heavier. Her arms and sides were in agony and her stomach felt like it was tearing, but she was just grateful she'd had the belt on her gown. She was certain she wouldn't have got the case out otherwise.

Finally, she reached the top of the incline, shuffled back and yelled as she pulled the case up and onto the flat floor in front of her. The tunnel was a little wider here, but Rose was still shivering and feeling sick.

A few minutes later, she could feel her feet dangling as they emerged from the tunnel entrance and she dropped them onto the floor of the cellar. As she pushed herself out and upright, she spun around but the room skewed, and she fought to remain standing.

'Thought you'd started burrowing and kept going.' Bloom's dark frame reared into view.

Rose tried to focus on him, but the lights were too bright again.

'I hit hard rock when I excavated the tunnel. Had to dig under it. That's why it's so steep. Thought it easier for you to find out for yourself. Any problems?'

Rose stumbled sideways but managed to save herself from falling.

'OK, just catch your breath a minute. I'll pull this the rest of the way out.'

She staggered over to the wall, aware of how warm the freezing cold cellar felt to her. She still had the lantern in her hand. She closed her eyes and opened them again; she could just make out Bloom leaning in at the mouth of the tunnel.

A sliding sound as he started pulling out the case.

She could slug him now. But her arms were shaking, and she could barely grip the lantern in her dead fingers. Her forehead prickled cold.

The case clicked as it was rested gently on the floor.

'Two down.'

Rose leaned over and threw up her pizza and red wine. Most of it streamed through her nose and left its burn there.

'You OK?'

She stood upright and felt the rest of her blood drain out of her head.

'I think you need to sit down.'

Rose shook her head, held her hand up.

Bloom waited.

Open your eyes.

She did and they gradually filtered the light. Bloom had a genuine look of concern on his face.

Rose took a breath and then took the key from her pocket. 'Now we're going upstairs.'

Bloom took in her open dressing gown. 'I think you need to collect yourself first.' He mimed wiping at his mouth as if she should do the same.

She pulled the gown around her, but couldn't secure it because her belt was still attached to the case. 'Now. You promised.' She felt like she was about to pitch forward. 'Noah!' It seemed to take all her energy to call his name.

No response from above.

His eyes darted for a few seconds. 'You're right. I promised.' He ambled to the bottom of the staircase. 'I'll open the door, just for a minute.'

Rose didn't move.

'You're going to have to give me the key though.' He extended his hand.

She'd been waiting to see if he'd forgotten and used his

own key to open the door. Perhaps this was still a deceit. She walked over to him, concentrating on each faltering step.

He took it from her. 'You're wilting. You need watering.' He turned and stomped up the stairs.

Rose craned her neck after him, but he kept his back to her as he unlocked the door. She could see the blade of the bread knife jutting out of his back jeans pocket. Was he deliberately showing her that? She couldn't work out if he'd used the key she'd just given him or another. The door opened and he leaned through it. She could hear a dull thump from the other side.

Bloom swivelled his head to her. 'He's fine.'

'Let me up there.' She put her hand on the banister to support herself.

Bloom nodded and turned away briefly.

Rose heard the key being taken out of the lock.

'OK.' He returned his attention to her and beckoned her up.

Rose ascended and Bloom stepped through the doorway to give her some room.

When she reached the top, she froze and her stomach heaved again as she caught sight of Noah.

He was lying face down on top of the packing case they'd been using as a table. He was gagged with a dirty white rag and had been hogtied with blue plastic-coated rope. He fixed her with a look of sheer terror, eyes bulging as the bonds securing his hands to his ankles strained tight. The pizza box they'd been eating from earlier had been swept to the floor and half-eaten slices lay around the tiles.

Bloom walked around behind Noah. 'Some children can't follow simple instructions but Noah's a credit to you. I told him not to try and move from here...'

Raw anger detonated now. 'Untie him! He can't breathe like that!'

'He's been fine all this time. Let's get you some water.'

'Noah, look at me, honey.'

He attempted to turn his head to where Bloom was but shot his terrified eyes back to her.

'Just look at me. Not him.' She tried to keep the tremor from her voice. 'Breathe slow like we did earlier. I'm not going to let him hurt you. Understand?'

He didn't blink, whimpered and strained against the ropes.

'Tell me you understand.'

He nodded quickly.

'You don't have to tie him like that.'

'I don't. Just a stickler for doing a job properly, I suppose. Water or not?'

Noah sniffed in hard and the handkerchief slicing into his mouth pumped in and out.

'The downstairs toilet.' She nodded towards the hall.

'You want me to get it from there?'

'Lock him in there.' Rose thought fast.

Bloom's attention shifted to it.

'There's a key in the door and there's no window. Absolutely no way for him to get out. Please… you know he'll be secure in there. And he'll be able to breathe.'

But Bloom seemed mesmerised by Noah's struggling.

Chapter Forty-One

'I 'm not going back down there until you do.'

Bloom still didn't shift his gaze from Noah.

'You can't expect me to leave him like this.'

Bloom eventually looked up and regarded her as if he'd forgotten she was there. 'I hear you.' He held up a hand as if he needed a moment to think. 'OK.' He nodded. 'Untie him and we'll put him in there.'

Rose didn't hesitate but crossed the room and started trying to untie the clump of knots at Noah's ankles. Her fingers shook but they were too tight to loosen.

'Let's move this along.' Bloom moved forward and the bread knife was suddenly in his hand.

'No!' Her hands shot out to shield Noah.

He slid the blade under the rope connecting Noah's feet and hands and started sawing vigorously through it.

Noah's body shook as Bloom worked his elbow faster.

Rose lifted her palms clear as he cut through the plastic, frayed the rope and then severed it.

Noah shoulders went forward but his feet remained curled up behind him.

'You hear your mother. Before I change my mind.'

'Come on.' Rose helped Noah off the packing case. He stood trembling, hands still behind his back and ankles still secured. She bent to remove the bonds.

'Leave those on him.'

She looked sharply up at Bloom. 'He'll be locked in the bathroom.'

'And he'll be sitting up. He can breathe easier now. I'll carry him there.'

'He can walk. You can shuffle there, sweetheart?' She started to take the gag from his mouth.

'Leave it.'

'He can't breathe.'

'Yes, he can. There's no pressure on his lungs now.'

'Just let me remove the gag.'

'No.'

'You can leave his hands tied. What could he possibly do?'

'This is the set-up or he goes back to how he was.' Bloom gripped the jagged end of the bread knife with his other palm.

Noah pleaded with Rose through the gag.

'I can't understand him. I'll have to remove it.'

'He's telling you he's fine. He's telling you not to push it. Right, Noah?'

Noah's wide eyes jerked to Bloom and back again. He nodded.

Rose restrained the words she wanted to spit at their captor. She couldn't provoke him when he was holding the knife.

Noah choked something else at her.

'Now he's saying he'll be cosy in the bathroom and won't make a sound.'

Rose kept her eyes on Noah. 'You'll be OK in there. I'll soon have you out. Understand?'

Noah held her gaze but didn't nod.

'Let's shuffle then.' Bloom gestured towards the doorway into the hall.

Rose put her arm around her son and helped him walk in tiny steps towards the bathroom. As they made their slow progress, she cast a look at the open cellar door. There was no key in it. Whichever one he'd used to open it was in Bloom's possession.

They reached the bathroom door and Bloom walked ahead of them to open it. He gestured them in.

Rose guided Noah to the closed seat, and he sat down on it.

'Out then.'

'But if he needs to go to the toilet…'

'He can do it right there.'

'Just untie his hands.'

'Negotiations are over. Out.' Bloom gestured with his head.

Rose turned and fixed her gaze on Noah again. 'I love you. Sit as still as you can…'

Noah's face remained rigid around the gag.

'I'll be back soon.'

'Rose.' There was remonstration in Bloom's tone.

Rose exited the bathroom and turned. Noah's petrified expression was sealed behind the door.

Bloom turned the key in the lock.

As he did, Rose acted on what she'd seen as they'd approached the bathroom. The closed front lounge door next to it also had a key in it. She'd left them in all the locks for the next owners. She quickly slid it out and dropped it into her right dressing gown pocket.

Bloom turned from the door and raised an eyebrow. 'Satisfied?'

Rose nodded, held Bloom's eye and prayed he didn't look down at her hand emerging from her pocket. 'Just sit tight. I'll be back for you soon!' she shouted past him to Noah.

Bloom didn't blink.

'Don't try to escape. Just do as you're told.'

'Is that advice you'll be following too?' Bloom leaned back on the door. He still held the bread knife in his right hand.

Rose nodded again. She could feel the weight of the key in her dressing gown pocket.

Bloom took the key out of the bathroom door, slipped it into his back jeans pocket and then angled his head at her, his neck folding in the process.

Had he realised she was hiding something? 'You'll be

safe in there. I promise!' But it was a hollow one. Bloom was still very much in control. However, Rose had already thought of a way of using the wrong key to escape.

'After you then.' He gestured theatrically towards the cellar. 'I've been as good as my word.'

Noah shouted something at her through the gag.

'Please, let me take that off him.'

'Maybe we can talk about it when you bring out the next pieces of luggage.'

Rose wobbled over to the door. She still felt light-headed and clasped the wooden banister as soon as she reached the top of the staircase.

'Do you need me to help you?' His voice was suddenly at her ear.

She quickly descended and swivelled at the bottom to look back up.

Bloom closed the door behind them and turned to it, but his back was blocking what he was doing. Deliberately?

She heard the key click and the lock shoot into place.

A few seconds after, Bloom faced her, key in his hand. But he'd had ample time to switch it. He displayed it in his thumb and forefinger as he came down.

Rose backed away towards the anteroom. She could smell the sourness of her pool of vomit, and it made her feel nauseous again.

'You've gone very pale, Rose. Maybe you should sit down a minute.'

'No, I want to keep going…' But cold stung her temples and she rocked on her heels.

'Put your head forward, get some blood into it.'

The room rotated and she reluctantly complied, taking in a deep breath. But the aroma of her sick was overpowering.

'It looks like you'll blow away any minute. Sit cross-legged before you fall over.'

Rose found herself sitting hard on the floor. She folded her legs in front of her and held up a hand when he approached.

'I'll fetch you some water while you're in the tunnel.'

She shook her head and held out her palm firmly. 'No. You'll need the key for that, and I want it back.'

Bloom pursed his lips. 'Suit yourself.' He held out the key to her and she took it from him with her right hand and dropped it into her left empty pocket so it wouldn't jingle against the other one. The action looked awkward.

'At least take a breather. Better you recover here first than pass out when you've less oxygen.'

He was right. She had to collect herself before she went in again. She had the key now, but he could so easily have given her a different one.

Bloom took a couple of steps back, seemingly to give her some space, but then turned to the second suitcase she'd brought out. He looked down at it thoughtfully. 'This was my best friend.'

Rose detected a trace of wistfulness.

'He was the one person who could see me.' He rolled his eyes to Rose. 'And that was something I couldn't allow. His was the only death that was one hundred per cent premeditated. The others were all improvised. That's the beauty of being invisible. I can remove people on a whim.'

Chapter Forty-Three

'He didn't struggle, just acquiesced. And there was a very good reason for that. I wrapped a length of extension cord around his neck and pulled tight. Watched his bald head go bright purple and his bony shoulders gently jerk. Held him like that for a good few minutes. Only released him when I felt alone.'

Rose felt the room start to right itself as Bloom walked a slow circle around the case. 'His body slumped forward onto the kitchen tiles and his face hit the floor with a pop... broke his nose. It was a shame. He'd been sharp, smart, somebody I felt was on the same level as me. Not something you encounter very often. People are generally predictable, transparent and stupid. They all underestimate me. That's what I rely on. My best friend saw past the cut-out that I hid behind though. I still wonder if that had been my fault.'

She felt her cheeks flush but knew she would struggle to stand. Again, Rose considered how explicit Bloom was being with her. Did he presume his confession would never go further than her?

'After Pam Grant, my confidence ballooned. It took a few months but when I was positive the police weren't going to come knocking on my front door, I started to polish the memory of what I'd done. The sheer randomness and the audacity of my action was what I fixated on more than the actual act and its aftermath. How could anybody find her? I had absolutely no motive for killing her. She was a stranger to me. And she was hidden away in a place only I knew.'

Rose heard a thump from above which cut off her breath. Was Noah trying to get out of the bathroom? *Please. Don't summon Bloom back upstairs.*

Bloom continued regardless. 'It was that knowledge that I valued most. I was the last person Pam had seen but her brain cells were now putrid mush, her motionless lips rotten elastic. No other witnesses came forward. I'd got away with it and the ease with which I had staggered me. It elevated my mood and outlook – permanently changed who I was.'

Rose anticipated another thud. Bloom had to have heard the first. Was he choosing to ignore it because he knew Noah couldn't get out?

'Suddenly I had a social life. A group of friends with whom I actually felt I belonged. I agreed to drinks after work and then a few trips to the local bowling alley. I joined a cycling club and that was where I met my friend. I don't like to use his name now. It doesn't prompt any remorse, but it's a reminder of an enjoyable period that's now over and done with.'

Another bump overhead.

Rose gritted her teeth. *Stay still, Noah.*

Bloom blinked rapidly as if he were listening intently but no other noise came. 'He was of a similar build and weight to me, so we usually ended up riding together. At that point, I felt one hundred per cent secure. I enjoyed belonging but hadn't connected to anyone I met up with. I could effortlessly appraise each person and know exactly what I had to do for them to allow me into their confidence. It was too easy. And it had started to get boring. Was this really what I'd been missing? My best friend was a different proposition though – a challenge. Whenever I thought I'd got a handle on him, he did or said something to confound me. It was because he was hiding something as well. He'd killed somebody. Not in the way I had Pam. My friend had only been seventeen at the time and had been learning to drive his brother's car. A child had run out into the middle of the road. Not his fault. But it had been him in the driving seat. He hadn't even been going very fast, but it had been sufficient to shatter an eight-year-old's bones. He'd never got behind the wheel of a car again after that.'

Rose winced as the bathroom door shook upstairs. Was Noah trying to boot it down with his bound feet?

Bloom waited for the sound to stop. 'He didn't share his guilt with me for a long time. When he did, though, I realised it was the closest I'd ever get to talking to someone who harboured a secret as terrible as mine. So I shared too. And planned to kill him immediately after.'

Rose was too alarmed by what her son was doing to fully comprehend the coldness of Bloom's admission.

'I was curious to watch my friend's reaction to my murder of Pam and the horror on his face immediately reinforced two things for me: One, I would never meet anyone like myself. Two, being the only one who knew about what I'd done was actually the thing that I enjoyed most. There was something else that nibbled at me though. My friend had truly seen me. Something not even my family could lay claim to. Perhaps it was because I'd let my guard down too much, in order to win his confidence. Whatever the reason, I could never allow it to happen again. Having somebody see who I was made me supremely uncomfortable. Even brought on panic attacks. They only stopped when my best friend was dead. And by then—'

Bloom paused as a series of bumps interrupted him.

Stop, Noah. Please, stop.

'By then I'd grown tired of my new friends and withdrew from my social life as quickly as I'd embraced it. In no time, I'd become invisible again. I'd enjoyed satisfying my curiosity, but now I was as safe as I'd been before. The only drawback was that Pam was no longer my secret. Even after I'd disposed of my friend, it felt as if my private memory of her death had been sullied through sharing it with him. I had to make another perfect memory. One that remained sealed inside me. It was an inevitability. I'd known it as soon as my best friend's suicide had been declared.

'Even though his body was never found, it was the likeliest explanation. He'd threatened it in the past. How could he live with the memory of hitting that girl with his car? The secret was out of the bag. I was the only member of the cycling club to attend the memorial. And while I'd commiserated and talked in hushed tones to his family, who were still waiting for him to turn up in some ravine, I had no immediate plans to take anyone else. Not until the perfect moment presented itself.'

Bang!

Stay still, Noah.

Irritation registered on Bloom's face and a deep frown settled in as he fixed his attention on the ceiling.

Chapter Forty-Four

R ose struggled to her feet but tottered when she was
upright. She had to distract him.

'You're still looking green around the gills.' Bloom
folded his arms.

She wasn't sure if it was concussion or his relaying the
casual murder of the person inside the suitcase, but her
head swam.

Bloom gauged her expression. 'He's going to be moved
to a better place now though. With the others. As I
mentioned, I'm something of a completist.'

Rose couldn't process the idea of there being more
suitcases like this somewhere else. Had what had happened
here only been the beginning? She put both hands in the
pocket of her dressing gown and shivered, steeling herself
for what she planned to do.

'Sometimes, bad things happen to good people.' There

was genuine sorrow in his tone as he looked down at the suitcase.

While his attention was off her, Rose grasped the key to the front lounge and slid it out of her right pocket. His gaze was still tilted down so she quickly switched it to her left hand.

Bloom looked up.

Had the movement caused him to look? There was no suspicion on his face. 'I'm not going back in the tunnels.' She shook her head categorically.

Now there was puzzlement. 'I thought we were singing from the same hymn sheet?'

'Please don't make me. Just… take this key back…' She put her fist in her left pocket and pretended to retrieve the key she already had in her hand from inside it. 'Unlock the door and let us go!' She hurled the key at him but made sure she struck the wall opposite the staircase.

Bloom watched as the key bounced off the bricks and came to rest a few feet away from the wall. He blinked rapidly. It was definitely a reaction he hadn't expected.

'Why are you torturing us like this?' She tried to imbue the question with hysteria. Was he buying it? Did he believe she'd just thrown the key he gave her?

'How is this display helping Noah? You're wasting my time and his.'

'Open the door'—she nodded at the key—'take these cases with you and walk out of here. I swear we won't call the police.'

Bloom's face darkened. 'We've been over this.' He frowned hard, his eyes still on the key.

Was he going to go for it? She needed him to pick it up. As soon as his back was turned, would she have time to cross the cellar floor, climb the stairs, unlock the door and lock it from the other side? He might not be in any hurry to pursue her if he thought he had the right key to the cellar door.

His pupils darted back to her. 'You've seen Noah. You have to take us to the next stage before you get another request.'

He still hadn't moved towards the key. Would he tell her to pick it up?

'If you need a few more minutes of breathing time, I'll grant it, but I think Noah needs to breathe a little more than you do.'

She still felt dizzy but nodded her head as if she were about to pass out to sell it even more.

'You're not thinking clearly.' His head turned back to the key and he paced over to it.

Rose maintained her position but filled her chest.

Bloom reached the key and bent down to pick it up.

Rose rocketed across the concrete floor and reached the bottom of the staircase. Out of the corner of her eye, she saw Bloom stand sharply upright. Not hesitating, she bounded onto the third step up and quickly ascended the remaining ones. Her hand was already in her left pocket and her palm closed around the cellar key. Would it be the right one or had he switched it too?

No movement from behind her. No sound of footsteps following.

That would change as soon as she started rattling the key in the lock. She held it firmly, but her hand was shaking as she attempted to slot it in. The metal scraped as she did.

'Rose!'

But his voice was still in the cellar. Rose turned the key harshly to the right.

'Rose!' His voice was more urgent, and the staircase shook as he pounded up after her.

Chapter Forty-Five

R ose felt the key turn and the lock snap out of the doorframe. She had no time to be relieved and barged the door with her shoulder and was through into the hall. She pulled the key out, closed it, put her weight against the panel and knew she had only seconds to lock it.

The thudding on the steps reached the top.

Rose missed the hole with the key and the end of it scraped around as her hand shook. *Focus. Lock it.*

The key slid in and she turned it but, as she did, the door butted her hard as it was bulldozed open from the other side. She was flung back as Bloom entered the hallway.

She clutched her arm, pain shooting through it, but remained upright as he blocked the frame so she couldn't close it again. It was the first time she'd seen genuine panic on his face.

'Where are you going to go now, Rose?' But his eyes flitted about her as if he might have overlooked something.

Noah shouted through his gag and the door.

'I'm interested, as I've got the key for the bathroom, how were you going to get Noah out before I booted down this cellar door?'

She'd planned to topple the pillar of boxes by the kitchen. The tools were in the bottom one and there was a lump hammer in there. She'd hoped a few blows would have broken the lock and she and Noah could have made a run for it before Bloom got free. She shook her head, as if that was something she hadn't considered.

Bloom continued to glance about her. 'So this key…' As he caught his breath, he held up the one she'd hurled.

'From that door.' She pointed to the one she'd taken it from. With Noah still locked away, it was too late to try anything more. Whatever the consequences were for her escape attempt, she had to try and mitigate them.

There was no anger on his face as realisation sank in. A half smile briefly played over his lips. 'Very resourceful.' He took a deep breath in.

Was this her only chance? If she let him take her back into the cellar, he was going to make doubly sure she wouldn't get another.

'Ingenious, in fact,' he conceded, nodding.

Where was the knife? In his back pocket again? Could she make a dash for the kitchen and try to grab another?

But something dark bulged in his eyes as the smile evaporated. 'That key was a gesture of trust.'

Noah yelled again.

Rose's eyes shifted to the bathroom door. 'Everything's OK!'

Bloom shook his head. 'No. I can assure you both, things are far, far from OK now.'

Rose met his gaze again and saw a raw malevolence bleeding through that opened a cold hollow in her. Thoughts of fleeing or attack halted.

'You're doing the best you can for Noah. You're his mother, I understand that. But there's no chance that either of you will live past tonight. I've tried to make things comfortable for you, but by abusing my trust, you've just removed any filter I might have put in place to make you believe you have a chance of seeing your son again.'

He wasn't trying to scare her. She'd known it was the truth and now he felt no reason to hide it. He would get what he wanted and then kill them.

'How difficult you make your last hours is your choice. More importantly, how difficult do you want to make Noah's last hours?'

She knew her son would be listening through the door and how petrified Bloom's words would make him.

'He'll be the first I go to, so you can listen.'

This is your last chance. Run to the kitchen. Get a knife.

But she briefly hesitated. She saw him now. Behind the

jocular façade, she could see pure evil. Something Rose had never encountered before. It restrained her.

'I'll dispose of you both down there. Seal it all back up. I'll leave just enough activity in your brains so you'll know that you've both been buried alive.'

Rose turned and headed for the kitchen, but she already knew it was pointless. His arm crooked around her throat before she'd taken her fourth step.

She felt his breath warm at her ear as he held her before blackness crowded in.

Chapter Forty-Six

When Rose opened her eyes to pitch blackness, she realised her mouth was full of cold dirt. She gagged and raised her head, but it immediately struck a familiar wet ceiling. She was underground and her hands were pinned below her.

Her son's name was the first word from her lips, and she spat out grit as she tried to draw in a breath. She stirred her muscles.

Where was Noah? How long had she been here? Was she tied up?

Her hands were dead from where her weight had been resting on them, but she managed to wiggle her fingers and start to pull them from the icy floor under her chest.

She felt pressure on her feet and her face was suddenly in the mud again. It covered her mouth and she had to lift it clear and puff out the soil as she realised she was being shoved from behind.

'This is as far as I take you.' It was Bloom's voice close behind her.

She could feel his fingers gripping her feet through her slippers as he pushed her forward again.

'You're in the collapsed tunnel that runs under the lawn. It was the roomiest one before the cave-in but now you'll have to do some burrowing to get to the last two cases. Just so you remember, I've got easy access to Noah so don't think of heading north to escape. Bring out one piece of luggage to me at a time.'

'Noah!'

'Concentrate on the job at hand.'

'Not until I've spoken to him.' She spat out more dirt.

'No more goodwill,' he retorted flatly.

'I won't do this until I've spoken to him.' She tried to flex her shoulders against the tight space.

'No?'

Searing pain shot across the back of her right calf muscle and Rose cried out.

'Each time you delay, I'll pass one of those back to your son.'

The breath caught in her constricted chest and briefly Rose couldn't speak. She choked back the agony. 'Please, I don't care what you do to me.'

'Yes. Blah, blah. My life for the kid's. Do I need to emphasise how far past those sorts of niceties we are?'

She felt him half remove her slipper and then felt the jagged metal blade across the sole of her bare foot. He pressed it in hard.

Rose tried to shake her leg free from his grip, but he held it firm.

She gritted her teeth, anticipating the teeth sawing into her skin.

'Crawl, little worm.' He released her ankle.

Rose dragged her feet as far up to herself as she could but felt the blade briefly prick her heel. Her cry stuck in her throat.

'The lantern is in there with you. Use it.'

She pulled her hands all the way out from under her and scrabbled about for it. 'I can't...'

'Look harder.'

She tried the space to her right but found nothing.

'It'd be difficult to lose it.'

Rose's hand butted the light as she ran it down her left side. She slid it up to her and shakily turned it on. Her space was illuminated and harsh clouds of her breath pumped around it.

'Progress,' Bloom commented sardonically.

Ahead of Rose was a wall of loose collapsed dirt. Did he really expect her to dig through that?

'I'm going back to wait for you in the cellar. Take too long and I'll go to Noah for some company,' Bloom threatened. She heard him slide back there before the silence closed in on her.

Chapter Forty-Seven

R ose felt the sensation in her right calf fluctuate between cold and warm. She was definitely bleeding, but she couldn't tell how badly. She tried to push the sensation to the back of her mind and dragged herself forward. She had to get the cases. They were the only things she could barter with.

She considered how he hadn't tricked her when he'd given her the cellar key. Would she be in a better position if she hadn't tried to deceive him? She doubted that. What she would do when she got back to the cellar she didn't know. Bringing out the final case meant she no longer had any bargaining power. How could she delay that?

She paused and listened, hoping to hear what was going on in the cellar, but it was useless. She sank her fingers into the loose mud piled in front of her and scooped some handfuls back towards her. Soon there was a pile against her chest that was almost up to her chin.

Rose slid over it, reached further forward and repeated the process. But was she blocking her own exit? Reversing through the piles was going to be difficult. It was the only option, however, and she'd just have to deal with that on the way out.

She couldn't contemplate escape, even though she knew the lawn was somewhere above her. She could only hope to return to the cellar with the cases and plead for Noah's release.

As she burrowed out some more loose soil and slithered over the next pile, the tunnel opened out and she was lying inside a section that was still intact. Rose shoved the lantern forward and it illuminated a coiled piece of navy-blue material. It was the belt of Noah's dressing gown. This was where Bloom had had her son tied up while she'd been in the other tunnel. It looked like the whole passage was falling apart. Rose seized the belt and pulled it back to her.

She inhaled the material, and the smell of Noah immediately filled her eyes with tears. She briefly closed her eyelids. What was happening behind her? Noah had already been through such a traumatic ordeal that night and she still couldn't hold his hand and protect him. As a tear cut a path through the grime on her face, she felt a fresh wave of hatred for Bloom.

Rose wrapped the belt around her right hand. Maybe she could dress her wound if she found a space large enough to examine her leg. She slid through the intact area of the tunnel until she came to a bigger pile of collapsed dirt. This had to be about where Bloom had dragged Noah down from the lawn.

But as she dug out handfuls of mud from the wall in front of her, more of it rolled down and filled in the small gap she was opening. There was no way through. She clawed it away faster but there was still no visible progress. Her shoulders shook with the exertion, so she rested her face in the cold earth pile before her, her fingertips pumping against the soil under her nails.

Rose felt exhaustion taking over. Heavy darkness slid forward from the back of her brain. She lifted her head and stretched her eyelids open. Was this the concussion? She turned to shout over her shoulder. 'There's no way through here!' She waited.

'Never say die, Rose. I have every faith in you.'

'I'm telling you it's impossible! The more I dig, the more it's crumbling!' Rose raised her eyes to the ceiling of the tunnel. If it were that unstable, it could cave in on her at any moment. 'I'm coming back out!'

'Not without the cases!' he retorted.

Rose racked her brains. If she got trapped in here, Noah would be on his own with Bloom. 'We could dig down from the lawn! If you know roughly where the tunnel ends, we could bypass the collapsed ceiling and pull them up from there!'

Silence as Bloom considered it.

'There's no way through!' she reiterated.

'I've only got your word for that, and I already have trust issues with you.'

'Throw my phone down here. I can take a photo!'

'Now wouldn't that be convenient.'

'Tell me what I need to do!' She inhaled through her nose, attempting to fill her crushed lungs.

'Do you have a spade?'

Rose felt a brief surge of hope. At least now they would have to move out of the cellar. 'Yes!' She had to keep making herself valuable to him.

A lengthy silence.

'OK. Come back out and we'll go upstairs together.'

Chapter Forty-Eight

After pocketing the dressing gown belt, it felt like it took Rose half an hour to renegotiate the piles of dirt she'd left in her wake. When she eventually dropped her feet onto the floor of the cellar and turned, there was no response to her cry from Noah. She touched the skin on the back of her calf and waited for her eyes to adjust to the glare of the room again. As well as wet mud, there was thick, dark blood on her fingers.

'You really are caked.' Bloom was standing in the shadows at the foot of the stairs, his back against the wall. 'Filth is definitely the new black.' He weighed the bread knife in his right hand.

'Where's Noah?' Her eyes scoured the cellar.

'He's secure upstairs.'

'In the bathroom?'

'Upstairs,' he answered shortly.

'Let me quickly speak to him.'

He shook his head. 'He'll be fine. As he's the only man of the house, he has to toughen up.'

That cut short her next plea.

'It must be difficult managing his upbringing all on your own.'

A chill set in her stomach. Rose had first assumed that she and Noah still being in the house when Bloom had called in had been bad timing. 'How long have you been watching us?'

Bloom cocked his head and pursed his lips. 'This was my home. I took an interest in everyone who lived here. Particularly as I left such a large part of my past behind.'

Rose wiped some dirt from her eyelashes and grains of soil fell from her hair. She recalled the intruder Lucas had found looking in through the hallway window that night in 2019.

'I told myself I could seal it up. Walk away from that part of my life and start over. I did for a while. Just to prove I could. I thought about the people living here and what they were unwittingly sharing with me. But they were only passing through. Why *would* they find the bodies? When you moved in, I thought it would be the same again. But then something tragic happened, didn't it? Something that trapped you here.'

Rose's eyes briefly shifted to the top of the stairs. Was the door unlocked? Bloom must have taken the key from the cellar door after he'd overpowered her but had he sealed them down here again?

'That's when you had to step up. I know Lucas's little pottery workshop didn't exactly bring home the bacon but suddenly your earnings were the only thing holding this house together.'

She met his eye.

'I've been there. In fact, I've been here. I know how many bites a place like this takes out of your finances, particularly as you had Lucas's healthcare bills to pay.'

Had he been watching them since the day they'd moved in?

'What was it that put Lucas out of action?'

The more terrifying thought was that as Bloom had been observing them for a very long time, he'd obviously planned for tonight and knew exactly what he'd do with them.

'I saw him in the hospital.'

'When?' Rose asked, dazed.

'Early days. I'd followed you to St Austin's. You were visiting and you left Noah at a school club while you did. You met your younger sister there. You both sat with him, distraught. I walked into his room afterwards. He was still in a coma. Not that his current condition is much better. It was after visiting hours and a nurse chased me out. Not my proudest moment.'

'She wasn't my younger sister,' Rose interrupted him.

Bloom frowned, as if surprised she hadn't reacted more to his disclosure.

Was it true that this man had been lingering on the periphery of the most traumatic event of her life? 'She was his lover.'

Chapter Forty-Nine

All these months later, the anger was still raw. It was twelve months to the day since she'd started drinking again. She'd come home from the hospital after hearing the final results of all the tests they'd done on Lucas and been given his prognosis. She'd abstained from alcohol for seven years before that because she didn't want to end up with her mother's problem, but she'd opened one of Lucas's bottles of red wine that evening and drained it. Since then, she'd been fooling Noah into believing she only did it at weekends.

'Does that fill the blanks in enough for you? My husband was in bed with his student when he had an aneurism. The last words he spoke were to *her* in a cheap hotel room less than three miles from this house.'

Bloom didn't react.

Rose tried to halt the usual playback in her head. How

Lucas complained he was having one of his thunderclap headaches that morning but how he said he needed to finish a couple of commissions in the workshop that day. He must have left the house for the hotel his student was staying at as soon as Rose had driven out of the drive for the school drop-off. She'd headed for her surgery in Petworth General as usual and he'd met Jane Trent. Just after eleven o'clock in the morning, he'd had a seizure. He'd been in bed with Jane, and she'd been the one with him in the ambulance and holding his hand in the hospital while Rose had been oblivious. Jane hadn't phoned her until mid-afternoon.

'He was with another woman?' Bloom shook his head.

'So you think my son needs to be tougher? Let me see him. I'll get you both the cases, just let me know he's all right.' She interlocked her fingers into a fist at her chin and gritted her teeth. She had to remain calm. Had to be thinking straight if she was ever to get her son away from Bloom.

He rocked forward and stood upright. 'Does Noah know?'

'Know what?' Rose snapped back. 'That his dad may never be able to speak or use his limbs? That he may permanently need twenty-four-hour care? Yes, he's still coming to terms with that.'

Bloom looked briefly chastened.

She suspected it was an act though and that he was enjoying tormenting her. Was he coaxing things out of her he already knew?

'Does he know about Jane?' he asked, mock innocently.

Rose narrowed her eyes. 'No.'

'So, you're still protecting him?'

She nodded, unsure where he was directing the conversation.

'What from? Who Lucas was?'

There was no levity on his face now. Rose glimpsed the darkness in his eyes again.

'From the idea that when you both looked away, Lucas was far from the honest father you thought he was. That barely beneath the family veneer lived someone with a secret and a need you couldn't fulfil?'

Rose realised he was entranced by their exchange. He'd been drawn out and away from his jovial disguise. Was this more valuable to him than what was in the cases? 'He's lost his father. That's already too much for him.' Why was she explaining herself to him?

'So when *will* you tell Noah?'

It was a question she'd asked herself a hundred times.

'Never?'

'I haven't decided.'

'But at some point in the future, you'll most probably destroy Noah's image of Lucas?'

'I told you—'

'Because he'll have to know the truth, as you have. Is that what you're telling yourself?'

'Yes!' Rose knew he was baiting her but felt her control slipping.

Bloom blinked thoughtfully. 'Or is that the ultimate revenge on your part? The idea that you both sit there with Lucas and hold his limp hand and your cheating husband knows that one day Noah's going to look at him differently because of what you will eventually tell him. Is that the power you have over Lucas now?'

A ball of rage expanded. 'Fuck you. You don't know anything about my family.'

'Nor do you,' he said dismissively. 'If you did, you wouldn't have had to share your husband's bedside with another woman.'

Chapter Fifty

Bloom had first seen Jane at the hospital, as Rose had the day she'd got the panicked call from her about his seizure. A twenty-one-year-old that Lucas had been sleeping with. Rose had smashed every piece of pottery in his workshop when she'd got home. She hadn't been able to bring herself to throw the fragments away though. They were all boxed up too. She fought against everything she wanted to yell at Bloom. It was what he wanted to hear. She wasn't about to give him the satisfaction. 'Noah!'

Bloom cast his eyes up the stairs as they both waited for a response.

Nothing.

'Answer me!'

Bloom folded his arms in the silence.

'Why isn't he answering?'

'Maybe he can't hear you.' He shrugged his shoulders.

'He can. Even through the cellar door.'

'You're misunderstanding me. Maybe he can't hear you.' He raised his wiry eyebrows.

Her fury was instantly doused. 'What have you done?'

'What have *I* done? You're the one who betrayed the trust we had.'

Rose took two faltering paces towards him. Pain shot through her calf. 'Tell me!'

Bloom held up the serrated blade. 'He's probably already deceiving you.'

'What are you talking about?' she spat, but halted where she was.

'It's what boys do. It never fails to amaze me how parents refuse to credit their offspring with the guile they had as kids.'

'Noah! Shout back to me if you can!'

Bloom gave it a few beats to allow the quiet to register before continuing. 'There'll already be secrets he's keeping from you. It's what boys do.'

'Stop this.'

'Small cruelties to begin with. Burning ants with a magnifying glass – entry-level stuff.'

'Take me upstairs.'

Bloom didn't budge from his position. 'We quickly learn how to present the person our mothers want to see and know exactly the things we need to keep private.'

Rose tried to collect herself. Maybe her attacking him was exactly what he wanted.

'And where do we learn it from? Our parents. Especially our mothers. Withholding secrets.'

Rose's feet started moving her closer to him.

He didn't react. 'Deception. We all learn to do it from an early age.'

She turned her attention to the foot of the stairs.

'And it seems like Noah's had a good teacher.'

His words were in her right ear as she turned and started to climb the staircase. She anticipated his hand restraining her, but he didn't move as she limped up them. The door would be locked. She was sure of it. 'Noah, answer me!' She took hold of the handle and turned.

'Isn't that right, Noah?'

The door gave and swung out. She could see the passage, the empty lounge and the open bathroom beyond. But Rose didn't step over the threshold. She turned back to Bloom.

He was still in the same place and his focus was on the bottom of the stairs.

'OK, buddy. You can make a noise now.'

Rose was briefly frozen where she was as it dawned on her what he'd done.

'Can't have been easy, but better it comes out now than her hiding the truth from you any longer.'

Rose came shakily back down. Bloom had used the hiding place she had for the first case. She looked around the side of the stairs and suddenly was gazing into Noah's terrified and gagged face.

Chapter Fifty-One

'I told him he had to be quiet as a mouse. No matter what he heard.'

'Noah.' Rose tentatively approached her son, her relief overcome by what she knew he'd heard.

'Don't be angry. He was protecting you, Rose. I told him you'd come to terrible harm if you knew he was there.'

Rose sank to her knees behind the stairs. Noah's wrists were still tied behind his back and his ankles secured. Her fingers went to his gag.

'Don't.' Bloom's voice was behind her. 'I'm surprised you'd even want to hear what he's got to say to you now.'

Rose gripped Noah's shoulders and looked into his glistening eyes. She could see something else there other than fear: a dismay, a deep disillusionment. 'Darling, listen to me…' But where could she begin?

'Looks like Daddy wasn't the only one being dishonest.'

She shook her head at Noah. 'You're too young to understand.' He'd heard everything.

'Just twenty-one. That's the age your father's girlfriend was, Noah.' Bloom sighed.

Rose whirled round to him, her hands still clutching Noah's shoulders. 'Bastard!'

'In front of the child? This is turning out to be a real baptism of fire for him.'

Rose couldn't find the words. He'd pretended not to know who Jane Trent was, but it had all been a ploy to draw out the truth in Noah's presence. How had he known?

Bloom looked fixedly down at her. 'One of Lucas's pottery pupils. Such a cliché that you never believed Lucas could do something so obvious.'

He knew every detail of Lucas's betrayal.

'Brought a little extra income into the home so you never questioned it. Even when you saw the girls who were coming into the house as a result.'

'That's enough!' Rose didn't want Noah to hear another word.

'I told you I took an interest in everyone who came to live here after me. I was sad to hand the front door keys over, but I was sure to have copies made before I did. It's an old place. Locks have never been changed. Nobody's ever had any security fitted. I just let myself back in whenever I wanted. I might glance at some opened mail. Switch on a laptop and find the passwords in the leather notebook in the top desk drawer.'

It was Rose's notebook he was referring to.

'It's easy to extrapolate a family dynamic with what you can piece together from those. I always did it when the house was empty. To begin with anyway. But with Lucas working here, I got bolder. I could have held a party when he was locked in his pottery workshop. Particularly when he was in the middle of teaching. I listened to him and Jane. To be fair to them both, they never used your bed.'

Rose turned back to Noah and covered his ears. 'Don't listen to what he's saying.' But it was too late.

'I knew about Jane before you did. Listened to their conversations about Lucas's guilt. That's why they started meeting in the hotel. He paid for that room because to him relocation outside the family home meant he was cheating less. It made a skewed sort of sense to him, I suppose.'

She shook her head at Noah, and he closed his eyes.

'I don't think he would ever have walked out on you and Noah, Rose. I'm convinced he would have come to his senses and let Jane go eventually. The aneurysm was just bad timing. Maybe, in a weird way, it makes what happened to him more bearable for you though. Hard to imagine how painful it would be to visit him in hospital if you still believed he was the faithful husband and father he'd led you to believe he was. We all deceive. And it's a salutary lesson about the consequences we have to pay when we do.'

As she tried to process what he'd told her, one thought was paramount – this was how he'd deliberately decided to chastise her. 'And what about the consequences for you?' She didn't turn to him, couldn't look at him.

He didn't reply.

'Tell me, if we all deceive, how have you ever been punished?'

Chapter Fifty-Two

'I don't indulge in deception.'

Rose tried to stem the emotions within her: anger, mortification and shame all vied with the hatred she felt for her tormentor and how he was getting a kick out of using what he'd learnt while he'd been casually walking in and out of their family home. But could she play for time by indulging him? 'You deceived me when you told me Noah was upstairs.'

'True, but only because you tried to trick me. I'm just punishing one deception by using another and I can't think of a better way of making my point.'

She turned sharply to him. 'What about the people you've murdered?'

Bloom narrowed his eyes. 'What of them?'

'You must have deceived them… to lure them.'

'No,' he stated simply. 'I told you, they were spur-of-the moment, utterly unpremeditated.'

'Even the man you called your friend?'

'That was a necessity. But there was no deception. He knew exactly who I was before he died. And I didn't "lure" him. I don't "lure" people. I just recognise a chance and take it. It's what I always do.'

'And when you attended his memorial and were talking to his family. What was that?'

Bloom rolled his eyes briefly up and nodded as if her point were valid. 'I gave them my condolences. That was heartfelt. He was a good person who would be missed by his brother and parents. I didn't deceive them by being there. I wanted to show my support.'

'For the man you'd strangled.'

'Nobody ever asked me if I'd done that, so I never had to lie.'

She couldn't see a flicker of amusement on his face. He clearly believed his own twisted logic.

'Nobody's actually ever asked me if I kill people,' he added.

'And what if they did?'

He pursed his lips, pondering it a moment as if he never had before.

Rose's eyes darted to her son. If their dialogue *had* bought her time, then she didn't know for what.

'If it was self-preservation, I suppose I'd have to dispense with my scruples. But it's not a situation that's

226

arisen yet, so I can still afford to take the high ground on this one.'

Another sickening thought occurred to her. 'Were you ever in this house with Noah?'

'I largely visited in the day. Obviously with Noah at school…'

'Were you ever here with him?' she demanded.

Bloom inhaled through his nose and nodded. 'One Wednesday, I think Noah was on half term. You weren't here but Lucas was. He was busy in his workshop, actually working and not focused on his extra-marital activities. Noah was in his room on his laptop. Headphones plugged in and oblivious to everything else. I stood outside his room and watched him through the cracked door.'

Rose shuddered as she imagined Bloom in such close proximity to her son.

'I slipped into your bedroom when he came out to use the bathroom. I went through your bedside drawers. I didn't find much to indicate you were a very creative couple between the sheets.'

Rose shook her head – she couldn't summon the words of disgust she felt for him.

'But I know Lucas kept a stash of ribbed condoms in his workshop. They were nothing to do with you though.'

'Just shut up.' Rose didn't want Noah subjected to any more revelations about what she'd protected him from. Her palms were still covering his ears. But Bloom clearly wasn't finished.

'Maybe that was why he sought Jane's young company instead.'

'Do you want me to fetch the last cases or not?' Rose realised her hands were tightening around Noah's head. She released him.

'Rapid subject change.' Bloom looked down at Noah. 'You can't always brush these things under the carpet.'

She followed his gaze to her son. His eyes were still shut tight. She couldn't shake the image of Bloom having been so close to him and what could have happened.

'But if you're up to it... let's head upstairs.'

Chapter Fifty-Three

'He goes first.' Rose nodded at Noah.

'He goes nowhere.' Bloom dipped his head towards the stairs to indicate she should move.

'Please.' Rose bent her shoulders forward and just resisted clamping her hands together to beg.

'Do you really want him privy to any other little confessions you might have?'

'Just move him somewhere he's comfortable.'

Bloom shook his head. 'I'm locking him down here.'

'Will you give me the key?'

'No.' His expression was implacable.

There was no reasoning with him. Rose touched her son's shoulder again. 'Noah.'

He didn't open his eyes. They were screwed tightly shut and tears glistened on his eyelashes.

She couldn't conceive the emotional distress that had

been inflicted on him and what effect their ordeal already had. 'Listen to me, just sit with your back to the wall, OK?'

He eventually nodded and shifted his body so his shoulders were against the dusty bare bricks there.

'I'll be as quick as I can and then I'll come back for you.' But she'd said that when he'd been locked in the bathroom. He probably knew as well as she did how powerless she was. She felt her own tears but fought them back. 'Open your eyes and look at me.'

He did and they told her he didn't believe her.

Would this be the last time she saw him? She had to do something to alter the outcome and fast, had to seize even the tiniest chance. She had Noah's dressing gown belt coiled up in her pocket. She imagined trying to throttle Bloom's thick neck with it, but her strength was no match for his. 'You know how much I love you, don't you?'

Noah's face was frozen.

'Noah, you know how much I love you.'

He nodded once.

She bit down on her emotions. 'Everything I ever do is to protect you. And I'm not about to stop doing that. Do you understand?'

He nodded again.

Rose leaned forward and kissed his damp, cold forehead.

'OK, this is all very Hallmark Channel but I'm going to have to insist.'

Rose stayed kneeling but spun her face to him. 'He's just

a child. When did you become such a monster? What the hell happened to you!'

Bloom had his palm extended to the stairs. He lowered it and sighed slightly. 'Noah's lucky to have such a protective mother. Aren't you, Noah?'

Rose didn't turn to see if her son reacted. Had she touched a nerve? She had to proceed carefully. 'Is that what you need?' She softened her voice. 'Or is that what you needed in the past, someone to protect you?'

Bloom's eyes slitted as if he were reading her obvious motives. He whispered when he answered. 'You'll fight for him, won't you? Tooth and nail and to the last breath in your body?'

She nodded her head once. 'Only you can stop this.' Rose wondered if pandering to his ego was the answer. 'Only you have that power.'

He considered it. 'My mother could have stopped it. Any time. She never did though.'

Rose swallowed. 'She hurt you?'

'There wasn't a time I can remember when she didn't. Before I was even out of the cradle. Bruises, cigarette burns. That's what she dressed me in every day.' Bloom's eyes seemed to engage with the memory. 'I thought that was how your mother was meant to act. Thought it was completely normal.'

Rose stood. 'I can't even begin to imagine a life like that.' She tried to meet his eye, but his attention was on Noah.

'It was only when I started playing with other kids that I

realised how wrong my childhood was. Nobody got punished like I did. Nobody got shut away or beaten blue the same way. She was meant to be my protector.'

Rose held her breath, considered how to react. Did everything hinge on what she said next? 'That's the way it has to be. Nobody has the right to harm a child like that. Your mother betrayed everything that should have been natural to her.'

Bloom rolled his eyes to hers.

Rose could see the aggression there and stiffened.

But then Bloom's expression erupted into a broad grin. 'I'm just pulling your chain. My mother doted on me. In fact, she probably spoiled me rotten because she knew I could never compete with my brothers. I miss her every day.' He blinked. 'Now, if you're all finished psychoanalysing me, let's get on with this.'

Chapter Fifty-Four

R ose could feel Bloom's weight squeak on the stairs behind her as she hobbled up ahead of him. He'd lied and mocked her attempts to locate his vulnerability. His deception punishing hers again? It was pointless even attempting to reason with him. There was no humanity within Bloom and he could clearly pre-empt every emotional ploy she'd try. She could easily turn around and kick him full in the face though. But she was only wearing slippers. Could her size five foot really make any impact? She could probably give him a bloody nose, but it was unlikely it would knock him out. And even if she had time to barricade the door with a chair, that left him alone in the cellar with Noah.

If she was to dig down through the collapsed tunnel to get the cases, however, she would need a spade. That's when she had to be ready. She didn't doubt that she could bash his brains in. All that was important was that she made sure he didn't return to the cellar. Rose reached the top of the stairs and waited by the door.

Bloom creaked up behind her. 'Keep going.'

Rose limped a couple of paces through the open door towards the lounge.

'Stop there.'

She halted, looking at the stacked boxes. Every potential weapon was packed and out of reach. Where was her phone? Did he still have it in his pocket? It was raining outside, and the droplets blurred her view of the darkened lawn.

'Looks like it's going to be a swamp out there.'

Rose imagined the water pooling in the collapsed tunnel.

'Wait, we've left the lantern behind.'

'There's another one in the kitchen,' she retorted quickly, turning. Rose didn't want him going back down there.

'If you're sure?' He seemed unconvinced.

'Under the sink.' She nodded.

'OK.' He took the cellar key out of his pocket and turned to the door.

'Noah, be brave!' she shouted through the doorway.

Bloom pushed the door closed before Noah could respond and locked it. 'After you.' He indicated the passage of boxes.

Rose faltered through it and entered the kitchen. The light was still on and rain rattled on the skylight above.

She knew there were only a few blunt knives left in the drawer.

'Find it then.' His voice wasn't close. He was hanging back.

Rose bent to the cupboard under the sink. It had been emptied out, but she knew there were candles and an LED lantern left in case of power cuts. She found it and pressed the button to switch it on. A circle of light appeared on the kitchen floor around her.

'You're going to need to dig your way down quite a few feet.'

'There's a spade somewhere at the end of the lawn. An old rusty one the previous owner left here.' She prayed it was still there. When had she last seen it? Not when she and Noah had been fumbling around the edge of the grass in the dark.

'If you think it's good enough for the job.'

She nodded and rose, closing the cupboard door. Rose wondered if she could use the lantern as a cosh, but it was only lightweight plastic.

When she turned, Bloom's attention was on the rivulets running down the back door window. 'It's filthy out there. You're not exactly storm ready.' He eyed her muddy dressing gown.

It seemed such a ludicrous thing to say. 'Do you really care?'

His eyes were back on the window.

'Worried that *you're* going to get wet?'

'We'll wait a few minutes.'

'The rain could already be filling the tunnel.'

He held up his palm. 'Turn off the lantern for now.'

She did.

'It's a good job we left Noah where he is.'

'Why?'

'He doesn't need to hear the precise details about the people in these cases. I think you do though. If you're thinking of trying anything out there, you definitely need to know.'

Chapter Fifty-Five

'The decision had been made for me. Usually I identify an opening but, on this occasion, I knew I had no choice but to act. They'd both seen me. I'd been in the front driveway and had got up close for a look through the lounge window. When I peered through the glass, I found them both staring back.'

Rose rested her lantern on top of the draining board as Bloom fixed his attention on the pane and the memory beyond it.

'The light in the area was subdued; only a battery candle had been burning on a shelf at the back of the room and it had taken my eyes a while to get accustomed to the gloom. When they had, the man and woman were standing there, both frozen by my observation of them.'

Rose dipped her eyes to his right hand. It now held the bread knife.

'They may have heard me arrive in the car but that wasn't important. I just had to deal with them both immediately. I stepped back into the shadows by the front door and waited for them to respond. Would they call the police? That was very possible, but I counted on one of them coming out to ask what I was doing on their property first.'

She tried not to look at the drawer only a few inches from where she'd placed the lantern. Could she open it and snatch out one of the knives?

'Sure enough, I saw a figure appear at the front door's frosted pane as the porch light was turned on. It was the woman. She didn't open it, just asked if she could help me. It sounded like the last thing she wanted to do.'

But Bloom was already in possession of the sharpest knife. Rose doubted she could scratch him with the blunt blades, even if he let her get anywhere near him.

'I cursed myself for having made such a foolish mistake. I'd been sloppy – got out of the car on the opposite side of the street and strolled over but they must have heard my car door slam and watched my approach. There was no time for recrimination though. I said I hadn't meant to scare her and that I just wanted to speak to her husband. I needed to get them both in the same place so there was less chance of one of them escaping.' His eyes darted briefly to Rose.

She nodded quickly, as if she wanted him to continue, using all her willpower not to look at the drawer.

'She told me he wasn't her husband but called him

238

anyway. He was even more suspicious than her. Demanded to know who I was. He was making it really difficult. I had no weapon with me either. My visit hadn't been about that. I'd just been observing. He got more aggressive so I followed suit. Pitched myself higher than him and told him he'd pranged my car. That gave him pause for thought, especially when I said it had happened in the drive-through. I knew they'd just been there to pick up dinner because I'd been tailing them for about a quarter of an hour. I told them I'd followed them home because of the accident. Said I'd been given false details before and wasn't going to fall for it again.'

'You deceived them?'

Bloom sniffed irritably. 'I embroidered what had already happened.' He raised his eyebrows, as if asking her if it was OK to proceed. 'Neither of them were having a bar of it but I'd planted a doubt. They were both insistent they hadn't hit me.'

His gaze was back on the pane again. 'That was true. But they *had* just brought home burgers from the drive-through. They still didn't open the door.'

If she ran upstairs now, would he pursue her there or go straight for Noah?

'People like them are always suspicious so I decided to go on with my lie and told them I had witnesses. They just kept repeating that they hadn't hit me and that I was a trespassing this and a Peeping Tom that and that I should get off their property before they called the police. I was confident they wouldn't do that but then I saw why they were so cocky. They had a security cam doorbell. They were recording me. That meant I had to get inside and get hold of their phones as well as destroy the camera. It did give me an idea though. Told them I had dashcam footage of them hitting me.'

Rose wondered why he was delaying going outside. Did he really need to share the details of how he'd murdered them to frighten her or was there some other motive?

'Told them there didn't need to be any ugliness but that I just wanted their insurance details. And if they weren't insured that was OK and that we'd come to an arrangement. They refused flat but kept whispering to each other. It was going south fast so I told them to come out to my car and watch the footage if they didn't believe me. I thought I'd lost them then and I was already thinking about how I'd have to find a rear way in even though they'd both be on their guard. I turned and was about to leave, get in the car and drive away for appearance's sake. That's when the woman opened the door.'

Chapter Fifty-Six

'I saw the hostility on their faces before I punched the woman in the middle of the forehead. It felt like I'd broken my hand. The woman screamed at me and staggered back into the hallway. She elbowed the wall to prevent herself from falling backwards but she was stunned and disoriented so I lunged for the man as he tried to run.'

Rose could see that Bloom's eyes were immersed in the specifics of the memory.

'I caught him by the collar of the threadbare green jumper he was wearing and used it to tug him back. Landed him a blow to the back of his skull square on and he dropped to his knees. I quickly closed the front door and checked on the woman. She slid down the wall, fingers squeaking as she dropped onto her back. Her partner was crawling away on his hands and knees.

'I felt reassured then that I could handle them both, but I knew I couldn't afford to be complacent. There was a red retro phone on a shelf at the end of the hall so I walked past them, grabbed the whole unit and brought it down hard three times on his scalp.'

Rose tried to block out her repulsion and pictured Noah tied up under the cellar staircase.

'That quietened him down, so I turned my attention to the woman. She was getting up, trying to support herself against the wall. She asked me if Bootsy had sent me. I didn't have a clue who that was so I told her yes. She said he'd given them another two weeks to pay so I assumed he was a loan shark or their drug dealer. Having observed them for as long as I had, I knew the couple lived pretty hand-to-mouth. The man threatened me to leave her alone then. Very chivalrous. I struck him with the phone again and he didn't move after that. I stopped short of caving his skull in. Too much clean-up time. The woman stood up and her eyes were rolling back in her head. Looked like she was going to topple at any minute. She just kept repeating that they had two weeks left to pay. They didn't have two minutes. But then she offered to get me the money right there and then.' Bloom shook his head.

Rose was revolted by the amusement on his face. 'What had they ever done to you?'

'To me? Nothing,' he replied dismissively. 'But I had to exert some damage control. She told me she had the money in their bedroom. I knew she was lying but I waved her upstairs and followed her up there. I figured I could strangle her on the mattress and she'd be all ready to wrap up in the sheets. Halfway up, she turns and looks back at her partner but there wasn't an ounce of concern for him on her face. Only fear for herself. And, as predicted, she tried to escape as soon as she was on the landing. She locked herself in the bathroom.'

All the time, Rose knew he was waiting for her to make a move. But as soon as his story was finished, they would be heading outside so the time she had left to do so was shrinking fast.

'Took me three attempts to bust the door down and when I got inside, she wasn't there. The little window was open so I looked out. She was halfway down a plastic water pipe, and I was about to order her back in when it broke. She bellyflopped onto the concrete below. Landed really hard. She was motionless for a few seconds but then drew breath, moaned and turned on her side. She started making this terrible hissing sound, like she might have broken a rib and punctured a lung. "Wait there," I told her and checked the houses on either side. It was night-time so nobody was around and her screams for help were barely a whisper. But she'd started to crawl, on her hands and knees, over the concrete and onto the lawn. There was a fence at the other end of it with a gate into the alleyway and she was headed for that. Thought she could escape.' Bloom's eyes shifted to hers and back to the window again.

Was this the point of the story? Was the lawn the place where he'd chosen to finish her?

'I trotted back down the stairs, stepped over her partner and went to the kitchen. I selected a thick-bladed carving knife from the block. It looked cheap so I knew it wasn't going to be sharp enough to go in clean but that was on her. The back door was locked and there was no sign of a key, so it took five attempts for me to boot it out before it gave. I caught up with her just as she was trying to reach for the handle of the gate into the alleyway. Grabbed her hair, yanked her head back and stuck the thick, cheap blade into the side of her neck. It went in easier than I thought and I held her head until she'd stopped trembling. I checked the houses on either side again. Nobody heard her.'

And there was nobody to hear Rose. Not for miles. *Do something. Anything.*

'It was fortunate that I could finish her outside. The blood would soak away and would do so even quicker when I used their hose. I'd just started that when I heard moaning coming from inside the house. I couldn't believe he was still alive. He was talking gibberish when I got back to the hallway. As I finished him, the entire blade broke off from the handle and got lodged in his chest cavity. I couldn't pull it out. Cheap knives. I turned on a few more lights so I could find their phones and disable the doorbell. After I wrapped their bodies, I pulled the car into their driveway and loaded them up and then I went back inside.'

He sucked his bottom lip. 'You know something, I was so famished by then that I sat down in the kitchen and ate both their burgers and fries.'

Rose's hand shot out and yanked the knife drawer.

Chapter Fifty-Seven

The drawer was empty.

Bloom didn't even react. 'I've never been a subscriber to the Maccy D. Too synthetic for my taste. But, I must say, I could have eaten those two Happy Meals a couple of times over.' His voice remained level, his attention not shifting from the pane.

Rose took in the dirty white lining of the drawer. When had he emptied it out? Maybe it had been after he'd overpowered her and dragged her back into the cellar. He'd had ample opportunity.

'I'm actually feeling a little hungry now.'

Rose slowly slid the drawer shut. 'I could... make you something.'

Bloom turned to her and grimaced. 'Thanks for the offer. I'll grab some breakfast after.'

'After?'

He nodded, his expression unchanged. 'Yes.'

No pretence about her usefulness beyond digging up the cases. 'So, when I find them…' She gripped the handle of the lantern. It was now the only weapon to hand. 'What do you do with them?'

Bloom seemed mystified she'd asked the question. 'Take them out of here.'

'Where?'

'To a safer place,' he said offhandedly, then walked to the window of the back door and peered out. 'You know, I think it's actually stopping.'

Rose registered the rain was still falling as hard.

'Let's try and find this spade.' He unbolted and opened the back door and ushered her through.

Was he running out of time? Rose had no idea what time it was. She limped quickly past him into the cold air and the raindrops pelted her face. Again, she considered that the story could be false. Maybe she'd got all the cases he wanted and now he was going to dispose of her here. She recalled how difficult it had been trying to scale the wall, but she couldn't try to run when Bloom still had Noah locked in the cellar. She had to put him permanently out of action. As she switched on the lantern and shone it on the grass, her eyes scanned the borders of the lawn for large stones or anything else she could use against him. The glowing tent was ahead, and she knew there was still a knife inside. But how long would it take her to find it?

'So, you know where you can find it?'

His voice confirmed he'd also exited the kitchen but was hanging back behind her. He was referring to the spade.

'My son's inhaler is in the tent. Can I get it?'

'I said we'd never mention the inhaler again. Where's the spade?'

'I think it's leaning against the far wall.' She looked right and saw the collapsed tunnel where Noah had been grabbed. That seemed like days ago now. She highlighted it with the lantern.

'Keep your light ahead then.'

She returned it to the wall in front of her and as she approached, she could see the old spade. If only she'd grabbed that and brained Bloom when he'd first appeared from the tunnel.

'Fetch it and bring it over.'

She turned back, illuminating him. He was striding towards the collapsed tunnel.

He halted. 'Light in front.'

Rose swung it back to the wall and covered the last few feet of lawn. She took hold of the spade by the handle, which was coated with dried concrete. The length of the spade was covered in it too. The tool felt so heavy. Could she swing it with enough force if she got an opportunity? But Rose guessed that Bloom wouldn't give her any.

'Come and take a look.' Bloom was peering into the pit by the wall. He turned as she obeyed and then he stood back a few feet.

Rose hefted the spade in her right hand and held the

lantern in her other. If he looked away for a moment...
Smash it against his head. As many times as you can.

But his eyes remained fixed on her as she arrived at the edge of the collapsed tunnel.

She rested the spade, blade down between them, but it was no barrier if he decided to attack her. He still had the bread knife. Rose peered briefly at the deep puddle of rainwater in the bottom of the pit.

'How long can you hold your breath?' He wiped the rain from his brow and blinked while he waited for her response.

Her fingers clenched the handle of the spade harder.

His attention switched to her white knuckles. 'If you need to get that over and done with, be my guest. You're still going down there though.'

He was ready for her to use it on him. Had already dismissed her attempt.

'If you dig through the bottom, it should drain out the water and you can crawl through. The cases aren't much further than maybe eight feet that way.' He pointed to the end of the lawn. 'You'll know which is which.'

Rose didn't even notice the cold rain running down her. So, this wasn't a bluff. There were still two cases he needed. Once she was down there, could she crawl back to the cellar and untie Noah? They could head back into the tunnels to hide, and Bloom was too out of shape to follow them. Is that what he wanted though? He could seal them up, including the collapsed one. They'd never get out. Plus she hadn't been able to get through from the cellar side.

'You'll have to bring out one at a time. Push them as far out as you can, and I'll do the rest.' He took another pace back.

Now he was several feet clear of the spade and well out of harm's way.

She lifted the tool, set her lantern on the edge of the pit and stepped down into the cold water. It came to just above her shins.

'Dig down as far as you can in the same place,' Bloom suggested.

Rose took a breath and then jarred her shoulder as she dug the blade firmly into the mud at her feet.

Chapter Fifty-Eight

The first spade of earth came out with a squelch and the water immediately filled the indentation as she lifted it clear and heaved it onto the lip of the pit. Rose dug in again, harder and deeper, and felt the harsh impact in her wrists. The spade was twice the weight this time and she trembled as she swung it towards the rim. She couldn't hold it though and its load fell back into the water.

'Use your foot on the edge of the spade. Get as deep as you can.'

She could detect frustration in Bloom's voice, but he remained where he was. She jabbed the spade in again and tried to lift her right foot, but her slipper was now stuck in the mud. Her foot popped out of it and when she tried to slide her toes back in, she couldn't find the opening. What the hell did it matter? The thin soles of her slippers were no protection. She put the bare sole of her foot on the sharp edge of the spade and pressed down as hard as she could. Pain shot up her calf where he'd cut her. The spade went in half an inch but then stopped. She tried to reposition herself, but her left slipper was stuck now as well. She tottered and righted herself before she slipped her left foot out of the other slipper.

'You'll be up to your knees soon.'

He was right. The rain was falling harder. Rose wiped water from her eyelashes and rested her right foot back on the blade of the spade. She put her weight on it and felt it painfully indenting the sole, but the blade went further down. She leaned her weight on the handle and grunted.

'You've got this,' Bloom encouraged her.

The spade suddenly dropped half a foot. She was through. The level of water around her feet sank a little and then stopped.

'Keep going.' Bloom took a step forward but halted.

Rose lifted the spade and rammed it back into the water but the hole she'd just dug had filled in again. She chopped at it repeatedly, yelling with every strike and churning up the brown liquid about her ankles.

'Careful you don't cut off a pinkie.'

She ignored him, kept going and only stopped when she'd found the indentation she'd made. She put her right foot on the blade again and pressed down harder, tugging her left foot out of the mud and putting her whole weight onto it. She rocked her body from side to side and the spade sank. She waggled herself as it went lower, and the mud emitted a loud sucking sound.

The water drained out of the pit and disappeared in the open slit around the blade.

Rose stumbled back from the spade and her spine hit the edge of the pit. The last of the water disappeared like a plug had been pulled from a bath and now she could see her waterlogged slippers trampled into the mud.

'Dig down before it fills up again.'

Even though she now had her back to him, Rose registered that Bloom's voice sounded closer.

'You'll need a big enough space to push out the cases.'

She returned to the spade where it was lodged and yanked it out with her second attempt. Rose hacked at the earth and opened a larger hole, slinging the dirt out behind her and not caring where it landed.

'Careful.'

It sounded like she'd hit him, but she carried on regardless. A few minutes later, she staggered back, her chest heaving.

'That's still not quite wide enough.'

Rose was exhausted and leaned on the side of the pit.

'You're nearly there, Rose. Just take a breather and then finish it.'

But Rose immediately returned to the spade and kept digging, even though it felt like her heart was about to explode. Bloom had moved in range. Her arms pumped faster, spade arcing and slinging the mud out in his direction.

'Turn around and throw it out the other way.'

She didn't stop. The hole was big enough for her to slip through now.

'Rose…'

He was going to let her finish now she had a rhythm though. She dug in and got a good load on her spade and then whipped it at his face.

'Rose!'

It had found its mark and, as Bloom put his hands up to wipe it away, Rose turned, lifted the spade and brought it down on both his boots.

Chapter Fifty-Nine

Bloom howled and seemed momentarily suspended in pain, his body teetering as Rose lifted the spade away and then jabbed the edge forward as hard as she could into his shins. She felt steel impact bone. Bloom fell sideways and landed hard on his right shoulder.

Rose brought the flat of the spade down onto the side of his face and it made a dull thud as the metal battered his skull but, now he was low on the ground, it was difficult to strike him with any force from her position in the pit.

Bloom moaned and put both his hands to his head.

Had it been hard enough to stun him? Rose didn't hesitate and quickly scrambled out of the pit with the spade, holding the blade high as he rolled onto his back and extended his palms to protect himself.

'No!' For the first time, there was fear in his eyes.

She brought the spade down, the back of it crushing his

hands to his chest and the edge catching him on the bottom of the chin. As she lifted it away, there was a look of shock and a few seconds passed before he drew breath and the agony registered. A low guttural sound escaped him.

She'd already lifted the spade again and swung it down in the same place but this time the spade hit him flat on the face and the noise stopped. Lifting it clear, she could see twin streams of blood flowing from both his nostrils. Rose turned the handle in her muddy palms so the side edge would chop his head but as she moved forward and cleaved it downwards, he caught it with his hands.

Bloom's mouth opened because he'd clearly absorbed the force with his palms.

Rose tried to prise the spade from them, but he maintained his grip.

She twisted the handle and his fingers quickly released it. Maybe she'd broken them and that was why the pain was etched so deeply on his forehead.

Kill him. Finish him. Keep him away from Noah.

She rammed the blade against his throat.

Bloom gurgled and both his hands were on the spade again.

She leaned harder on it as his eyes bulged wide. Bloom pushed back, gritted his teeth and tried to wedge his chin down to repel the blade but she increased the pressure.

Bloom put both his hands on the base of the handle as she drove herself against it.

He grunted and lifted his shoulders a few inches from the ground.

Her weight wasn't going to be enough. She could see that register in his eyes. He looked at her unblinking and readjusted his grip on the handle.

She pulled back and attempted to tug the spade from his hands, but he wasn't letting go. She heaved and yanked on it but as she did, he'd got himself into a sitting position. If he got onto his feet, it would be over.

The panic had gone from Bloom's face, but he was still clearly in pain.

Rose stamped hard between his legs.

Bloom's body flinched and his eyes closed in agony as she pulled the spade from his fingers.

Now the fear was back in his eyes. She had to make this count.

She couldn't raise the spade too high because she didn't want to give him any time to defend himself, so she lifted it to get a hard enough blow and smashed it down. It caught his forehead and the impact felt hard, but his hands were immediately around the blade.

She attempted to free it, but he twisted his body, leaned on his side and kicked her legs from under her. Rose released the spade and landed hard on her front.

As she scrambled to her feet, she knew he'd already be on his.

Chapter Sixty

Bloom was upright, wiping the stream of blood from his nostrils. He was holding the spade and raised it high with his right hand as soon as she took a step back. He blinked hard at her and shook his head as if trying to focus on her.

Rose held out her shaking palms. If she moved, she knew he would strike her.

More blood poured out of his nose and over his tight white lips. His jaw was set hard and his whole frame trembled, his deep black pupils locked on hers.

She could see a large purple patch had quickly flowered above his eyebrows where she'd struck him with the metal, and he limped and blenched as he took a pace towards her.

Rose cowered and retreated.

'Stand still.' The blood bubbled on his mouth.

She nodded, held her hands to her head. But she didn't

doubt he could chop through them and brain her with one blow.

Bloom wiped more blood away with the dark sticky back of his left hand and then gripped the handle of the spade with both fists. His shoulders tightened as if he were about to bring it down.

'You told me to do it!'

His expression and position remained rigid.

'You told me to!' She flinched as she anticipated the blow. In a second, she'd be unconscious or dead and then Noah would be alone.

A snort of blood escaped Bloom and he lunged forward with the spade.

Rose dropped to her knees, hands over her scalp and eyelids clenched. She drew breath and, in the seconds that followed, wondered if it was her last.

The impact didn't come. Then she felt the cold metal rest lightly on her knuckles. Bloom patted them gently with the spade.

'Stand up,' he whispered.

Rose opened her eyes.

He tapped her knuckles harder. 'Up.'

Rose stood and met his gaze.

Bloom spat some stringy blood onto the grass. 'Thank you for the… impromptu makeover.'

But she could see the rage in his glare. He looked badly shaken.

He rotated his right shoulder. 'You still haven't finished

though.' He nodded back into the pit.

Rose shook her head. 'And after you have what you want, you kill me.'

'No.'

'Don't lie to me.'

'After I have what I want, I kill both of you.'

The matter-of-fact way he admitted what she'd always suspected was still an icicle to her chest.

'Do as you're told, and I won't kill you in front of him… or him in front of you for that matter.'

She felt the burn of tears, but none came.

The rain was washing the blood from his face now. 'I'm fresh out of mercy, Rose. However, I can promise to make it quick for Noah. After your abuses of trust, that's all I can guarantee now.'

Rose felt the ground swing beneath her feet.

'No time to faint. Yes or no?'

'You were always going to kill us,' she croaked and felt her circulation suddenly slowing.

'Admittedly. But what I didn't account for was your resourcefulness. That's been an education.' He nodded to the hole. 'That'll be caving in again soon and I'm not handing you back the spade.'

Rose wanted to collapse. Should she beg now?

'Thinking about it, Noah's much smaller than you. He could scramble in there lickety-split.'

A harsh gust of wind almost blew her over.

'That's not a half-bad idea, is it?'

Rose knew exactly what he was doing.

'Well?'

Rose breathed heavily down her nose.

Bloom raised a bloody eyebrow.

She trudged and limped over to the pit and jumped back into the muck. The hole she'd dug was still draining out the water.

'Five minutes. If you're not back with the first case in that time, I'm going to the cellar. Don't forget your lantern.' He kicked it from the rim into the pit.

She picked it up. It was still on but now caked in mud.

For a few moments, Rose gazed into the blackness of the hole she'd dug. Then without taking a breath, she put her hands through and leaned in, letting gravity do the rest.

Chapter Sixty-One

As her shoulders slid through the slick mud, the darkness enveloped her. Rose felt her whole body slide inside. She just wanted to keep falling, be suspended in that moment so that the inevitable couldn't happen, but moments later she was shocked awake. She was face down in cold water and she had to lift her mouth out to drag in a breath.

'Five minutes starts now!' his muffled voice warned.

Some of the brackish liquid went down her throat, and she angled her head higher as she tried to pull her hands up from underneath her. She was still holding onto the lantern, but her weight was pinning it under her breasts. She dragged it painfully clear and the light flickered and went out. Rose was in pitch darkness. She frantically tapped it. Nothing. Had the water got inside? She tried to rise but her head was immediately against the ceiling of the collapsed tunnel.

Keeping the lantern out of the water with both hands, she wriggled her body so she had both her elbows supporting it and rapped the plastic casing again. To her relief, it came back on. In front of her, she could see the length of the tunnel that was still intact bending around to the left. The light flickered. Rose held her breath and was relieved when it didn't go out again.

She blinked moisture out of her eyes and squinted ahead. There was no sign of the cases. Were they even down here? But Rose suspected Bloom would have killed her with the spade if they weren't. She kept the lantern above the water level with her right hand and used her other to drag herself forward. He'd said the cases were only eight feet forward from where they'd been standing. The tunnel ahead became tighter, and she had to duck her head as she squeezed herself further in.

She'd only succeeded in wounding Bloom, but Rose still had one slim chance of saving Noah and that was dependent on her getting to the cases. The tunnel behind her that led back to her son was blocked and, even if she could make it through, they would still be locked in the cellar. What was Bloom doing while she was down here?

'I can't see them!' she yelled and waited.

'Say again!' His voice sounded distant.

But Rose was relieved he was still there. She needed to know he stayed outside. 'I can't see them!'

'They can't have gone anywhere! One lady's, one gent's!'

Rose had reached the bend and shone the light into the space beyond. There they were, stacked at the end in a raised recess. A grubby pink Samsonite case on top of a black one. 'I've found them!'

'Bring them out one at a time!'

She wondered which was the more valuable to Bloom. The body of the man or the woman? Or did he merely perceive them both as property to be returned? Rose moved the lantern forward and the cases were bathed in brighter light. She had to dip her head under the water to clear a collapsed section of the mud ceiling above and held her breath as she did so, quickly squirming through. But she dropped down into a trough.

Rose's waist got stuck halfway and she couldn't negotiate herself any further. She tried to lift her face clear of the cold water but gulped some of the brown liquid. Twisting her waist, she frantically attempted to free herself.

It was no use. She had to go back. But her legs couldn't get any traction. She was stuck and now she sucked more of the water into her nostrils. If she didn't move, she'd drown. Rose tried to lift her head higher, but the level was still over her mouth and nose.

She released a panicked exclamation and thrashed her hips against the sides of the tunnel. She was grazing the skin off, but she didn't care if she had to break a bone to get clear. More water got dragged into her mouth as she tried to inhale. She spluttered, expelled it but couldn't get a breath in between the next gritty mouthful.

Releasing the lantern, she dug both hands into the mud floor, put her face against the bottom and straightened her body as she tried to haul herself free. She could hear the sounds of her panic locked inside her skull as she flailed and tried to turn herself in the crooked space. She kicked her legs and rotated and as she released a scream, she shot forward into the upper end of the tunnel. Pulling her face out of the water, she took some short sharp breaths as her chest heaved.

'You OK down there?' It sounded like he'd put his mouth into the hole. His tone seemed almost concerned.

He was, of course. For what he wanted her to bring out. Would she be more valuable to him too once she was inside one of those cases? She didn't answer but was reassured that he was still present.

'Rose?'

She pushed herself up on her elbows. Now she was only about three feet away from the cases.

'Answer me.'

She could see light on the ceiling. Where was the lantern? She located it bobbing back the way she'd come and leaned back to grab it and then directed it at the cases.

'Your time's already up.'

'I've got the first one!' She shone the light back to where he was. 'But there's a—' She wretched and spat out some water. 'I'm going to need to open up the tunnel to fit it through. The ceiling has come down.'

A pause. 'It'll be light soon. How long?'

'Not long!'

'Don't play for time.'

'The case won't fit until I've made the opening bigger!'

Another pause. 'Do you want Noah to help you?'

'No!' she shouted back, her heartbeat lurching.

'If it takes longer than another five minutes, I'm going inside to get him.'

Chapter Sixty-Two

Rose turned in the direction of a sharp scraping noise behind her. Bloom had slid the spade through the opening.

'If you can behave yourself, use this.'

Rose figured she'd grab a case first and managed to hook her fingers around the handle of the pink one. There were only a few roots stuck to the side of it, so it came away with her first tug. She slid it longways and dragged it back the way she'd come.

Don't think about what's inside.

She found herself back in the trough, looked back to check the shape of the curve she had to negotiate and then shimmied on her side around it. She had to put her face into the water again as she went under the stalactite of mud in the ceiling but quickly emerged on the other side and secured the spade.

It was awkward carefully chopping at the blockage, but large chunks came away and she scraped them into the water and to the sides until the debris was dispersed. She prayed no more would cave in on her.

'You've had enough time now.' Bloom's face was at the hole again.

Rose had a weapon she could use against him, but he would certainly be expecting that. She had to bide her time and catch him off-guard if what she had in mind was going to work. 'I've got the first one here.' Rose slid back through the cleared trough and grabbed the handle of the pink case. It glided to her with a couple of tugs. 'Coming out now.' She saw Bloom's shadow shift as he stood back from the hole.

After several attempts to push the case through the hole, Rose's arms were trembling.

'Use the spade to open it up.'

She did as she was told but it was awkward operating across the case.

Rose tried again and this time the case fitted. It suddenly slid from her fingers as Bloom pulled it out the other side. She could feel the cold air rush in. It sounded like it was still raining hard out there.

A loud thud as Bloom dumped the case on the edge of the pit.

'Last one now.'

There was a lengthy silence as they both acknowledged the significance of that. It was the final thing he needed her to do.

'Don't delay. You've got a clear run with this one.'

Rose slid closer to the hole and found him looking down at her.

'Pass the spade back. You won't need it now. Handle end first. Slowly.'

Her hand was still tightly gripping it.

'Now,' he barked.

Turning the tool around, she pushed it out and he snatched it from her.

Rose heard it land with a clunk somewhere on the lawn. He'd tossed it.

Now that she had no weapon, he was probably feeling a little more relaxed.

'A few more minutes and we're done,' he said flatly.

Without replying, Rose slid out of his vision and frantically scrambled back down the tunnel to the final case. The lantern was still resting beside it, but the light had weakened. She examined the combination lock. Same number of digits as the one he'd opened in the cellar. She'd memorised the numbers as he'd done so. But would Bloom have a different code for each suitcase? Only he was going to open them, so why not use the same one?

Rose crawled closer and squinted at the numbers.

4869.

Her muddied fingers shook as she turned the tiny metal number wheels. She didn't have much time.

4869. She was sure that was the combination he'd used.

The last number slotted into place, and she tried the lock. It was still solid.

Were all the numbers aligned properly? She made sure they were all level with the line at the side.

Still, the lock didn't open.

Maybe he did use a different code for each suitcase. What the hell could she do now?

'What are you doing?'

Rose shook her head as she squinted at the numbers. The light from the lantern was fading. 'I've got it, but it's stuck!' she shouted back.

'You've got the same time to bring that one out or you know where I'm going.'

He knew that threat would be sufficient. Rose remained frozen for a moment. She knew it was 4 and 8 first. Had she got the second two digits around the wrong way? Her fingers readjusted the numbers. Maybe:

4896.

They slotted into position and this time the right lock shot open.

Chapter Sixty-Three

Rose spun her head in Bloom's direction. Could he have heard that? She returned her attention to the case and the second catch. Covering it with her palm to dampen the sound, she opened that one as well.

'Have you got it?'

Was that suspicion in his voice? 'It's not coming easily!'

'You've got strong arms. I've got the injuries to prove it.'

Rose winced as she dragged the case out from its resting place. Looking up, she estimated she had enough room to half open the lid. She gulped uncomfortably and lifted it an inch.

It wouldn't raise any further, so Rose had to angle the case slightly to allow it to clear the jagged ceiling. Now she could do it. Rose took a breath. Seeing inside was the last thing she wanted, but she had something worse to do.

Propping herself on her left elbow, she leaned forward

and reluctantly slid her right hand into the case. Her fingers skimmed cold plastic and ran over the contours of something solid beneath.

She took her hand back out as repugnance swept through her. She couldn't do it. Was Bloom's story about the knife blade remaining buried in the man's chest cavity a lie? And if it wasn't, might Bloom have removed it when he dismembered him?

'I need a bulletin, Rose!'

Bloom's yell reminded her she had no choice but to find out. 'I've shifted it half a foot. It's coming!'

He didn't reply.

Rose shook her head, gritted her teeth and slid her hand back inside the case. Her palm grazed the solid body part underneath it. She closed her eyes, let it rest on the shape.

The soft orange glow in front of her eyelids faded and went black as the lantern went out. She was in utter darkness.

She wouldn't stop now though. She thought of Noah tied up in the cellar. She was his only hope, and this was hers. She skated her fingers across the plastic, and they encountered a bump sticking up. Was that a nose? As she tried to grip it with her fingers, it seemed to collapse under her touch. Now she could feel a ridged circle of bone.

Rose wretched and bit down hard. She tried not to consider how decomposed the sealed body was as she moved her hands away from the bump and slid it to the left.

The plastic crinkled under her hand.

It encountered something larger, more solid. She squeezed it and her fingers sank into it through the plastic. There was something hard beneath. A bone. She leaned further forward and found the same shape there. Shoulders.

Rose's throat pumped but her hand was already moving downwards and soon her fingers were tracing the edge of a ribcage.

'You've got a couple of minutes left, Rose!'

She couldn't open her mouth to reply. She put her shoulder against the opening and ran her fingers over the torso until she found what she was looking for. The rough teeth of a zipper with cloth stitched on either side. But which end was it zipped from?

The booming in her ears reminded her that she should take a breath. She did so as she frantically sought an end or fastener.

'Rose?'

Sliding her arm all the way in, she found the bottom of the zipper. Nothing to release it there. She followed it over the bulk inside to the top end of the case.

'Rose?' His voice was close. He'd leaned further into the hole.

Her fingers found the zipper. 'I've got it!' she shouted back.

'I'm getting bored waiting. I'm going to check on Noah.'

'It's coming out!' There was no time.

'I don't see any sign of it.'

Breathing through her nose, Rose's fingers fumbled awkwardly with the zipper and tugged it down.

She heard the plastic relax and then the suitcase breathed out its noxious aroma.

Gagging against the putrid stench, Rose screwed her eyes tight and slid her hand inside the bag. She made straight for the ribcage, her fingers sliding over slick bones and scrabbling for the wet area underneath. Her fist became submerged in a cold, soft and slippery mass.

Rose didn't want to breathe but as her head pounded its accelerated countdown to unconsciousness, she pushed her hand in further. There was nothing there but the rotten tissue that broke against her fingers.

'Little worm?'

Bloom's voice sounded like it was right at her shoulder.

She lunged forward, driving her arm and hand further inside.

Something hard against her knuckles. A bone?

No. Metal.

Chapter Sixty-Four

R ose felt the sharp edge against the pads of her fingers. Bloom had been telling the truth. With a few tugs, the blade without a handle came free from the decomposed torso. She quickly pulled her arm clear of the case and it shut behind her.

Rose took a deep gasp of air through her mouth, but the fetor bled through her nostrils. 'It's here!' She quickly slid the blade into the right pocket of her soaking, mud-spattered dressing gown and then scrabbled for the lantern.

She found it, turned it off and on again and it flickered enough of its last power to show Rose her right hand was daubed brown to the wrist. Choking back nausea, she played the lantern over the catches and flinched as she locked each one again. She spun the combination numbers and then dragged the case out and up the tunnel.

Rose reached the trough of water and quickly dipped

her right hand into the brown liquid. She rubbed vigorously at it, but the slick coating remained there. She wiped her hand around in the wet mud to mask it and dragged the case over to the other side, ditching the lantern when it blinked and went dead.

She opened her mouth to tell Bloom the case was coming through but stopped herself.

Once he had the last one, she no longer had any use to him. If she gave it up that easily, he'd surely be suspicious.

As she reached the hole, Rose tried to slow her heartbeat and checked the blade was securely in her pocket. 'You're not having it until you've released Noah.'

No reply or movement at the hole.

'Can you hear me?' She knew he could. 'I want to see my son now.'

Still no response.

Had he returned to the cellar? That was probably what he wanted her to think.

Stay put.

But what if he *was* with Noah? He'd made his intentions clear. Rose moved closer to the hole. 'Answer me.'

'Push the case out.' The demand was softly spoken.

Where was he? Standing in the pit? Rose took the blade from her pocket. She would stab him as soon as she was close enough.

Don't hesitate. Heart, stomach, face, eyes – keep knifing him.

'Do it now, Rose. I've got the spade. Don't make me dig this hole wider and come in and get it myself.'

'It's going to be easier for you to fetch Noah than do that. Send him in here and I'll push the case out.'

'You know we're beyond that now, Rose.'

'But you're running out of time.' She gripped the metal. She was ready if he tried to lean into the hole.

'Why would you think that?'

'Morning's fast approaching.' Truth was, Rose didn't have a clue what time it was.

'This takes as long as it takes. Even if it's daylight, nobody can disturb us here. There's nobody to help you.'

'What about your truck? You don't want people to see it parked up.'

A brief pause. 'It's discreetly hidden.'

'And what about your injuries? You're going to need hospital treatment soon.'

'Look, I don't need any more complications, but the only thing that's really pressing is your commitment to pass out that case and have this over and done with for both of you.'

Rose shuddered.

'If you don't want to make this easy on yourself, make it easy on Noah.'

'You're just going to have to come in and get the case yourself.' She raised the blade but suspected what his reply would be.

'So, I visit the cellar first. You might want to join me there, but I guarantee it'll be too late for Noah.'

There was no playfulness in his voice. The threat was

definitive. He was tired and injured and out of patience. She had to use that.

'What *would* your mother say?'

Rose frowned. What new game was this?

'What do you think she'd tell you to do?'

She didn't answer. His voice sounded nearer. Was he moving closer to the hole? Rose's teeth started chattering as she held the weapon firmly.

'Not the best role model. More or less sat out her parental duties, wouldn't you say? But what would *her* advice be?'

Rose felt revulsion rise inside her. He didn't only know about her and Lucas. A new horror occurred to her as she repeatedly shook her head.

'Maybe ask her yourself. She's right outside. In this pink case.'

Chapter Sixty-Five

R ose's thoughts gridlocked and a few slow seconds passed.

'I often talk to my mother, even though she can't hear me. Sounds like you need the voice of common sense from somewhere.'

Dread bled through her. When had she last spoken to her mother? It had been months ago. She'd done her disappearing act soon after Lucas's seizure. Vanished with her new boyfriend, like she always did when things got tough. She'd been doing it all Rose's life and she'd assumed she would just reappear in a year or so and expect to pick up where they'd left off.

'But I don't think she really had that much common sense, did she? Maybe you'd be barking up the wrong tree.'

She always got in touch eventually with a new address and phone number because she'd ditched the last one so she wouldn't have her daughter calling and remonstrating with her. Rose had guessed she was getting the same treatment again. She'd been furious because her mother hadn't once accompanied her to the hospital to see Lucas. She'd figured her mother hadn't wanted to be confronted by the sort of infidelity that she'd been guilty of in her own past and fled. She was gone less than a month after Lucas's episode, when Rose should have been able to rely on her to look after Noah when she was visiting her husband in hospital. She still hadn't forgiven her – had been carrying the rage ever since.

'She only lived a ten-minute drive away, but I got the impression there was a greater distance between the two of you.'

This had to be an evil deception. He was trying to shake her up and lure her out of the tunnel.

'She wasn't around when you needed her the most, so I took some steps to remedy that.'

But now she was running back over the story he'd just told her in the kitchen about the couple he'd attacked in their home. Was that why he'd taken the time to tell her before she'd started digging? She draped his account over the house her mother had rented with her new boyfriend, Ray. The house that Rose had thought they'd abandoned.

'I'd followed them home from here before. Initially, from a distance, I couldn't fathom how they fitted into your life. It was a shock to learn she was your mother. Her boyfriend was so much younger. That's what threw me. I guess you never called *him* Daddy.'

He knew too much about her. Bloom had been an unseen presence in Rose's life way before Lucas had collapsed. Her eyes slid to the suitcase beside her.

'I was upstairs when I overheard you talking to Lucas about your mother and Ray. That's when I discovered why you kept them at arm's length and why you were always waiting to be disappointed.'

Rose suddenly became aware of her right fingers. The fingers that had taken the blade from the body in the case. They tingled cold as they gripped the metal.

'When I followed them home from the drive-through, I was only monitoring them. But then they saw me.'

Rose was standing in their driveway, visualising him looking in through their lounge window while they looked back.

'That was my carelessness. I had no choice. It wasn't something I'd planned to do then, but like every other time, the conditions were right, and I just acted.'

She imagined them opening the door to him and never standing a chance.

'I improvised but, all credit to her, your mother very nearly got away from me.'

Rose saw her mother lying on the lawn after she'd fallen from the water pipe and then Bloom coming back down the stairs and taking the knife from the block before he booted open the back door. The blade that was now in her hand.

'After I'd eaten, I decided to clean everything up. Take their phones and the rest of their belongings. I took those to the dump too.'

She sobbed as she saw him standing in the kitchen chewing their dinner while they both lay in the boot of his car.

'They didn't have a lot of belongings. I think they'd sold most of them to feed Ray's drug habit.'

Her mother had sworn on Noah's life she was clean, but she'd heard it all before and suspected Ray was using.

'I left the place spotless.'

It was how Rose had found it when she'd peered in through the lounge window as Bloom had. When she'd concluded they'd done the usual fast exit, she'd cursed her mother.

'And I brought them to the place they should have been. Home. With you.'

Her eyes were on the shadowy contours of the black case.

'You were staying with Lucas's parents. I knew you were taking Noah there for a week. That gave me plenty of time to install them here.'

Rose collapsed against the side of the tunnel.

'Where else was more appropriate? Maybe on some level you got comfort from their presence.'

Her hand clasped the blade tighter in her palm.

'I don't want to sound too altruistic though. I told you,

I'm a completist. If I'd known you were going to move so soon after, I would have taken them to the new location.'

She tried to recollect the last words she'd said to her mother, but she couldn't. However, she could recall how she'd internally vilified her as she'd driven home from her empty house. Her mouth tightened as tears stung her eyes.

'Maybe you'd like to see her again. Say goodbye properly. I can open the case up for you if you want.'

Chapter Sixty-Six

'Rose?'

His voice sounded closer now and she sat up and brandished the blade. The tunnel see-sawed as she tried to focus on the hole and blinked away tears.

'I'm going to the cellar now. Would you like to come with me?'

She opened her mouth, but her mind was numb.

'Your choice. You can make this easy or hard. Makes no odds to me. What do you say?'

She shook her head hard, trying to dispel the images and thoughts colliding there.

'Push the case out and you can come with me. Noah would want you to be present. I'm sure you can do a better job of being there for your child than your own mother.'

She wanted to fly out of the hole and jab the blade into

him, cutting and slashing him to ribbons for what he'd done.

'Let me have Ray now. He was never any good to you.'

Rose falteringly inhaled.

'Neither of them was. And if there weren't a blood bond, you wouldn't have cared what happened to her. Given their lifestyle, sooner or later, somebody was going to be finding their bodies.'

She had to stay in control. Even though she felt capable of anything now, Rose knew that Bloom expected it.

'Push him out. Let me take them both away from you.'

She just had to get close enough. But he wasn't standing at the hole. She had to think like him. Find the opportunity. He didn't know she had a knife. That was her advantage.

'And then we'll both take a walk to the cellar.'

He wasn't lying to her. He would kill Noah and her there and he knew she wouldn't want him to be alone with her son. Rose thought of her mother inside the pink case, her body sealed in plastic. Bloom had the same planned for them.

'OK then. I'll be back for you in a few minutes.'

Rose heard his feet squelch as they turned sharply in the mud. 'Wait!'

They stopped.

All Rose could hear was the rain still falling outside. She slid the blade back into her right dressing gown pocket and then leaned forward and shoved the case up to the hole. 'Take it.'

Bloom didn't reply.

'Take it!' She rammed it from the back so the front of it slid out of the opening. She pushed the case and waggled it and prayed she'd locked it properly. Did he already know? Had he heard her opening it?

The case was suddenly lifted from her hands as he tugged it out and she heard it land with a resounding thump.

She peered out of the hole and blinked as the raindrops fell on her face. There was no sign of Bloom, but she could hear noises of him scrambling out of the pit.

'Are you coming or not?' he asked.

Cautiously, she put her face through and located him. He was standing on the edge of the pit, crouching and poised to help her out. Did he have the bread knife ready and was waiting for her to get close too? He only had to cut her throat, push her back down the hole and fill it in with the spade.

He extended his right hand.

Rose emerged from the hole, the hard rain washing the mud away from her tear-streaked face. She eyed his other hand. It was at his side, but he could easily be concealing the knife. 'Step back.'

Bloom nodded and stood.

There didn't appear to be anything in his left hand, but he still had the blade hidden about him.

'All the way back.'

Bloom tightened his lips and nodded, as if he were

indulging her. He reversed three paces and then nodded at the case beside her. 'Slide it up with the other one.'

Her eyes shot to the pink case that was lying just a few feet behind him and she tried not to think about who was inside. 'Further away.'

Bloom kept walking backwards until he was standing in the shadow of the bay tree.

'Stay where I can see you.'

'Of course.' Bloom put his hands at his sides.

Without shifting her eyes from him, Rose bent and put her hands under the case and slid it up the muddy incline to the edge of the pit. It was too heavy and slipped back.

'Need a hand?' he offered.

Rose struggled with the case, her bare feet pedalling in the cold, wet mud. With a yell, she got it onto the edge of the pit and shunted it forward.

'Shall we get out of the rain now?'

Rose blinked against the droplets as she took him in. The purple mark to his forehead where she'd struck him with the spade had expanded and there was clotted blood about his nostrils. She'd injured and weakened him. Now she had to finish him.

'After you.' He gestured to the house.

Rose's attention was fixed on the pink case beside him.

Chapter Sixty-Seven

Bloom stayed where he was, a few feet out of reach. If Rose tried to attack him now, he'd be ready for her. She had to be ready for him. She'd done all he wanted and suspected he'd never needed her to load up the cases. She and Noah were just a loose end now.

He gazed down at the pink case too. 'D'you mind dragging her inside?' He looked up, cocked his head to one side. 'She's lighter than him.' He nodded to the black case she'd just pushed out of the pit.

Rose shook her head. She still didn't want to believe him. But there had been too many specific details to his story for it to be a lie. A giddying revulsion passed through her as she took in the case.

Bloom took a few steps back from it. 'Less of the histrionics though. You haven't even reported her missing.'

She wouldn't allow him to evoke a response from her.

Stay in in control. Nausea welled up in her. The case looked so small.

'I'll follow behind.' Limping slightly, Bloom moved slowly towards the black case, stepping around her and leaving the same gap between them.

She followed him with her head as he focused on the case.

He shot the handle out and tipped it forward to wheel it away.

Rose didn't want to touch the pink case. Not any part of it.

Bloom raised a wiry eyebrow. 'If you're ready?' There was fatigue in his voice.

He was moving Rose back inside and then down to the cellar. There he could kill her undisturbed. It didn't matter if she screamed right now though. There was nobody to hear.

'I guess this is what you call emotional baggage.' His eyes were blank.

It looked like she'd be expected to enter the house first. He would be distracted with bringing his case in with him and that's when she'd do it. *No hesitation.*

'Pick it up.'

Rose reached down and extended the handle of the pink case. It squeaked out before she tilted the weight. It didn't feel heavy at all. Rose wheeled the case towards the house, her bare feet squelching on the wet grass, head turned so she could keep one eye on Bloom's movement.

Bloom remained motionless, however, until she was nearly at the back door.

'Wait there,' he commanded sharply.

Rose could see him following her, hear the wheels of his case rumbling. She let go of the handle and it came to rest with a bump beside her.

His wheels halted as he stopped six feet behind her. 'OK, open the door.'

She obeyed, depressing the handle and letting it swing inside.

'Slide your case inside the doorway.'

She did so. Now she couldn't shut the door on him. But even if she did, what would she do next? Bloom still had the key to the cellar. She had to kill him to secure it.

'Step past the case and go into the lounge. You go anywhere else and I'm not coming to find you. I go straight to the cellar. Understand?'

She nodded her head once and then hobbled by the case onto the warm tiles of the kitchen. She turned left and entered the space between the stacked boxes. Now she was out of his sight. She lingered there, slid her hand into her soaking dressing gown pocket and felt the blade.

'Go all the way in so I can see you through the double glazing.'

She took her hand from her pocket again and padded gingerly into the lounge.

'Sit on the box there.'

Rose crossed the polished wood floor to the place she

and Noah had been eating pizza only hours before. She sat on the packing case and leaned her head on her hands. She was exhausted but needed Bloom to believe she didn't have any fight left. Her body was angled so the right pocket wasn't visible to him. Her hair hanging down over her knees concealed her hands. She could quickly pluck out the knife and run at him as soon as he entered the room.

'Don't move from that spot.'

She heard the second case being wheeled to the door and then a hissing as he moved the pink one with the black. Rose kept her head down, but her eyes tilted up to the doorway. Through the curtain of her hair, she could see her muddy footprints leading to where she was crouched.

The back door closed and then his footfalls crossed the kitchen tiles.

She had to wait until he was almost upon her.

He didn't appear though. What was he doing, taking out his knife?

Bloom slowly entered but lingered by the kitchen doorway at the other end of the boxes. There was nothing in his hands. 'You still with us, little worm?'

Rose emitted an involuntary sob that had been waiting to escape since his revelation about the cases.

He walked in a couple of paces. 'It's been a long night and I really do appreciate all you've done for me.' He continued forward.

Another five or six steps and she would go.

Chapter Sixty-Eight

A soft thump from down in the cellar.

Bloom paused mid-step and his attention shifted to the door behind Rose.

In that moment Rose sprang forward, drawing the blade from her pocket.

Bloom's hands were half up to protect himself when she reached him.

She aimed the blade directly at his chest and it struck something solid. The tip had made contact with the fingers of his left hand, but she drove it hard and it bounced and slid beyond them into his left bicep. She heard the metal penetrate muscle.

Bloom's yell was cut short by his sharp intake of breath.

Momentarily, Rose wanted to release the metal, but she tightened her grip and put her other hand on the blade as Bloom's right fingers tried to grab it and prevent it from penetrating further. She leaned her whole weight on the weapon and the thick blade slid all the way in right up to the hilt.

Bloom froze and then lashed out with his right fist.

It caught Rose square on the forehead and was enough to knock her back. She tripped and fell across the packing case where she'd just been sitting.

Bloom looked down at her with wide-eyed disbelief and opened his mouth. No sound emerged. He examined the blade in him, put his right fingers on the thin end and then held up his left palm to her, as if asking for a moment.

Rose sat bolt upright, anticipating another attack. She got to her feet.

Bloom didn't move, however. Breathed rapidly a few times and then started to slow it down. He gulped and released the metal. He looked up from it sticking out of him and closed his eyes.

Pull the blade out. Stick it back in his stomach. She hesitated.

In that moment, Bloom opened his eyes again. He seemed to identify the intent in her and shakily pulled out the blade. He gasped and took a faltering step towards her.

'Stop!' She had to block his route to the cellar.

Bloom reeled to her right but quickly regained his footing.

'Let me call you an ambulance.'

He snorted, amusement briefly filtering through the agony in his eyes.

'I promise… I won't tell them anything.'

He came at her, right fist drawn back at his side, ready to thrust the blade into her.

Rose yelled and twisted away from him, but the blade grazed her right hip as she stumbled towards the door to the front lounge. She twisted the handle and fell through. Turning on her back, she expected to see him in the doorway, but he wasn't there. Rose shoved the door with her foot, and it slammed before she got up and rammed her weight against it.

Breathing erratically, Rose waited for his bulk to batter her away.

No impact.

Why hadn't he followed her into the room?

A key turned and a door opened. *The cellar.*

'No!' Rose emerged from the lounge just in time to see Bloom disappearing down the stairs. He was halfway down as she stood at the top. 'I'm right here!'

But Bloom didn't stop or turn. He was going for Noah and moving fast, but his limp meant he was putting two feet on each stair.

Rose started after him, but he was almost at the bottom. Four steps down, she dived.

For a split second she wasn't sure if he would turn the corner before she reached him, but she slammed against his head and shoulders and her jaw connected with the back of his skull.

Bloom staggered forward, his legs taking quick steps to absorb the impact so he wouldn't topple over. Rose was still on his back. He lurched against the dartboard and his shoulder knocked it to the floor. He halted a few feet from the entrance to the tunnels.

She crooked one arm around his thick neck and clenched it around his throat.

His head angled to one side and his sweaty scalp was against her nostrils.

Pain shot up from her other hand as she realized he was biting the flesh between her thumb and first finger. A scream burst from her as the agony intensified. She could feel his teeth piercing her knuckle. Had he dropped the blade?

He furiously swung his body to try and shake her off, but she tightened her arm around his throat and tried to pull her hand from his mouth.

Bloom grunted as he bit down harder.

Her whole body tautened, and white light filled her eyes as he shook her harshly left and right.

Bloom growled and she could feel the heat and moisture of it on her fingers.

Rose tipped forward. He'd bent down swiftly and gravity did the rest. His teeth released her, and she landed face first on the concrete floor.

Chapter Sixty-Nine

Rose kept the canary yellow sleeping bag gathered at her chin but slid out of the zip door and stood up in it, shuffling towards her mother's tent that was pitched beside hers.

It sounded like her mother was crying again. She'd caught her in the past when she didn't think Rose was listening. But when she drank, there was no attempt to conceal it. It was distressing to see her like that – so vulnerable and oblivious to how it affected Rose. But now she'd seen it so many times she just went through the motions. Probably because she realised that the tears weren't for her father. It was self-pity. Her mother still hadn't accepted how much their life had changed. Rose had no choice but to become the grown-up.

The sound stopped.

So did Rose. Her feet halted their shuffle in the sleeping bag.

'Rose?'

She didn't answer. She knew her mother didn't want to see her like this.

Rose turned back in the direction of her own tent.

'That you?'

She started to pad back.

'It's OK. She's asleep.'

Rose halted and turned. Who was she talking to?

A murmur in response. A man.

Rose edged back.

'She won't hear.' The man's reassurance.

It was a smudgy voice. Just like her mother's after she'd been drinking the sloe gin she made at home.

Rose couldn't stop herself. Her father hadn't been dead five months.

As she parted the doors, she could see the impostor sprawled naked over her mother. Her mother's eyes opened. She saw Rose standing there, her dull regard on her for what felt like minutes while the stranger heaved away. Then she just closed them again, as if Rose's presence couldn't have been of smaller consequence.

Rose returned to her tent, lay down and pulled the sleeping bag over her face. Holding her breath, she tried to drown out the noises of her mother and the stranger and what they were doing behind the sound of the circulation in her ears, which pounded louder the longer she didn't breathe.

But she had to catch her breath and when she did, it seemed as if the plaintive sighs and encouragement her mother gave to the stranger increased in volume. Rose hated the need in those moans and whimpers. Was this what her mother wanted more than anything else? Was it more important than the memory of the father who had just been buried or the respect of her own daughter? Did everything her mother did lead to this and did everything else cease to exist in these moments?

The stranger said things to her mother that were mostly incoherent, but Rose understood their tone. He was promising her a release, making her voice her need for it and him. Rose felt ashamed for her and dreaded having to face her afterwards. There would be smiles of denial, soft promises of treats that her mother would be convinced were all that were necessary to distract her daughter from what had happened. Was this what being an adult was really about – seizing moments of pleasure whenever you could at whatever cost? The only time she saw her mother happy was when she was drunk or stoned. It must have nothing to do with her trying to forget she was a widow because that was how she'd been when Rose's father had been alive. There had been other men and Rose guessed she only knew the half of it. But now there was no semblance of respectability to maintain and her daughter's disapproval counted for nothing.

Eventually they finished and Rose kept herself trapped in the sleeping bag as the familiar aroma of marijuana drifted over. She tried not to hear his feeble excuses to leave. As she lay there, her hot breath landing heavily on her face, she vowed never to allow herself to be as vulnerable as her mother.

Part of her had always remained immobile inside the sleeping bag. She didn't realise that until a long time after. Not until she went out with her first boyfriend, and she found herself in what she perceived to be a predicament. It should have been fun; it should have been a discovery, but intimacy was an ordeal.

It was like that until she met Lucas. She never told him about the camping trip after her father's death. Never told anybody. The man who had been with her mother that night vanished like so many other men who followed. They came and went but Rose never allowed them to get remotely close to her. It caused a lot of friction with her mother over the years. It was why she'd agreed to move in with Lucas. She loved him but she knew she was escaping. They both wanted a child, so their intimacy was justified, even though she could never vocalise it.

Lucas had tried to be understanding but she couldn't even allow herself to be vulnerable with him. After Noah had been born, Lucas still wanted the intimacy, but Rose didn't.

She knew how difficult that was for Lucas. And when

she saw who his students were, she ignored the alarm bells. That's why she'd smashed up every piece of pottery in his workshop when she'd returned home from the hospital. She'd seen it coming for so long.

But as her ten-year-old self had held her breath in that sleeping bag, for the first time, she had heard her own voice so clearly in her head.

I won't be her. I'll never surrender myself.

Rose had listened to it ever since she'd heard her mother and the stranger goading her towards what he wanted.

'Just relax…'

That wasn't his voice now though. Who was that? So hot. Rose fought to compose her thoughts.

Bloom's yellow face was looking down at her. His lips were moving but the words seemed out of sync.

She tried to breathe but the yellow veil between them misted.

'Relax now…'

She could hear a buzzing sound nearby but when she inhaled, plastic clung tight to her mouth.

As Bloom's face emerged again from the white cloud, she tried to sit up but couldn't. Plastic squeaked as she attempted to move her limbs. She could see the tunnels behind him. They were still in the cellar.

Bloom's eyes shifted to a space on her left.

She turned her head and saw Noah lying on the concrete floor too. He was zipped inside a yellow plastic bag and her vacuum cleaner was attached by its pipe to the middle of it. His eyes were wide open, his mouth forming words she couldn't hear through the gag still in his mouth. The plastic clung tighter to his body as the vacuum sucked out all the air.

'Relax, Noah. It's nearly over,' Bloom placated him.

Chapter Seventy

Rose tried to sit up, but a heavy weight was on her chest. She looked down and saw Bloom's knee was resting against it.

'No!' She tried to turn onto her side, but his weight held her there. Her head swung back to Noah.

His eyes briefly rolled back, and his body jerked as he fought uselessly against his bonds. His shoulders were pushed forward so it was clear that his hands were still tied behind his back and pinned underneath his spine.

'Let him out!' She ripped the words from her throat and thrashed under Bloom.

But he increased the pressure on her. 'Ssshhh…' His attention was on Noah.

He was crushing her lungs and a breath was forced out of her, clouding the plastic again. She couldn't see Noah now.

'This is a first for me. I've never bagged anyone while they were still alive.'

Rose peered down at her hands. They were bound and resting just above her waist. She flexed her legs, but they were tied at the ankles. The bag she was inside was zipped up and the only air that could get in was through the hole above her waist where the vacuum pipe would attach. She rammed her fists against the rubber flaps and felt the cool air on her knuckles.

'That's an antique vacuum you have. It's really struggling.'

Rose bent her head down and put her face against the side of the bag below the condensation of her breath. She could see Noah still looking at her and chewing against the gag, but his eyelids were starting to close. 'Let him out! I'll do anything. Anything!'

'Thanks, but I've got what I came for. There's nothing more I need from you now.'

The plastic tightened harshly on Noah's face.

'Stop!' She shrieked and convulsed against the weight holding her to the hard floor.

Noah's faltering breath filled the tightening plastic mask and his face disappeared behind its fog.

'If you stop struggling, I'll do the same to you as quickly as possible.'

She tried to rock herself, to roll away, but she just bounced against the side of the bag as Bloom held it firm.

'You can't live with this now anyway. I'll use the

vacuum. Suck out all those bad thoughts and recriminations.'

Noah's body spasmed as the rest of the bag collapsed around him.

'The one thing I need you to know is that this was in no way personal.'

Rose tried to bore her way through, her face crushing against the tough plastic, her view of her son obscured by her hot, sour breath.

'You're just part of a random choice I made a long time ago. A preference. Like taking sugar in coffee. Nothing more than that.'

She couldn't escape and nor could Noah, but she kept driving her body against the barrier. She could see the twitching shape beyond her gradually slow.

'I think he's done.'

Her mouth opened but no sound emerged. Tears poured across the bridge of her nose and her head slid to the floor.

The only sound was the vacuum straining to remove any more air.

Rose felt the weight shift from her.

'Your turn now.'

Chapter Seventy-One

R ose could see his face start to rise above her. She closed her eyes, rallied her muscles and sprang upwards, aiming the crown of her head square at his nose. She didn't feel the impact. It only registered as a pulse of white light and a squeak of bone. She didn't care if she smashed open her skull. She had to damage him and as the cellar recomposed itself through a yellow haze, she struggled to process what she was seeing.

She was looking at Bloom's face through the plastic and his gaze was directed downwards. Rose prepared herself to headbutt him again as she tried to keep him in focus. He was slumped forward, the top part of his back against the wall and the rest of his body lying flat on the concrete floor.

She was on her knees. Her eyes darted from Bloom to Noah. The vacuum was still purring and the plastic around her son's body creaked as it shrouded him.

'Noah!' Rose ran her fingers up and down the white line that bisected her bag. Was the zipper at the top or bottom? Her attention returned to Bloom, but he hadn't moved. Was he about to come round?

She couldn't find an opening at the top of the white Velcro at her chin and slid her hands to the bottom of it. No opening there. The zipper would be on the outside. Even if she located it, she might not be able to open it from the inside.

'Noah! Answer me!'

Remove the pipe.

Rose rolled over to where Noah was and got back on her knees. She thrust her fingers through her vacuum hole to try and detach the vacuum pipe from Noah's bag.

Her fingertips touched it, but the hole wasn't big enough to get both her bound hands through.

The vacuum noise changed pitch as it emptied the last pockets of air from the wrinkled plastic.

She tried angling one set of fingers through but there was no way she'd be able to rotate the vacuum pipe. 'Noah!'

The knife. Find it. Bloom must have brought at least one of them into the cellar after the struggle upstairs.

She felt light-headed but tried to squint through the wet plastic for a sign of the weapon. Maybe it was in his pocket.

Bloom still hadn't moved. She scanned the floor of the cellar as she crawled in the bag towards him but couldn't see a trace of it. He had to have it.

Bloom's head jerked to the side.

She froze and waited. Had her cries to Noah woken him?

He groaned but didn't lift his head.

There was no time. Rose tried to work out the best way of positioning herself so she could search his pockets. But how could she do that if she could only get her fingers an inch or so through the hole?

He murmured and his open hand clenched closed.

Then she spotted the toppled dartboard. It was leaning against the wall a few feet from him, the number side against the wall. Rose slid over to it, sat down and used her bound feet to flip it sideways.

Out of the corner of her eye, she saw Bloom's body tense. He was waking up.

The dartboard had landed on its reverse side. The three darts were still in it where she'd replaced them. She crawled over to it and hovered the hole over the board. She lowered herself, grabbed the darts' flights with her fingers and yanked. Two of them came away.

Without checking on Bloom, she rolled back to where Noah was and lay so the hole of her bag was beside his face. His features were motionless and she couldn't see if his eyes were open or closed through the obscured plastic.

No time to worry about injuring her son. Rose pushed the points of the two darts into the plastic in front of his mouth with a low 'pop.'

The vacuum kept sucking out the air.

She stabbed again, felt the softness of the gag against the points as she repeatedly pierced it.

'Noah!' She screamed now. 'Noah, wake up!'

There was no response, no movement.

'Breathe!' She pushed her fingers hard against the opening and tore at the holes, making them bigger. She couldn't see Bloom, didn't know if he was already getting to his feet. 'Breathe!'

She opened a large rip around his face and the plastic around him started to relax even as the vacuum worked to close it again. Noah's eyelids were closed and motionless.

'Come back to me!' Her fingertips were against his clammy cheek. It felt so hot.

Noah's mouth opened and so did Rose's.

Her son took in a short breath and then a painful gasp. His eyes opened.

'Noah! Get up!'

He looked up at her and she could see the confusion in his expression.

'Try to crawl out.' Had the lack of oxygen damaged his brain?

But as he blinked and alarm returned, she could see he remembered where he was.

'Rip your way out! Quickly!'

But his eyes shot behind her, fear immediately registering.

A scuffing noise close by. Bloom was up.

Chapter Seventy-Two

Rose didn't turn. She had to get free and she had to lead Bloom away from Noah. Had he locked the door above? He must have gone to the hallway to get the vacuum. She walked forward in short steps inside her bag until she was at the bottom of the stairs.

Biting at the plastic rope knots at her wrists, she got them free before quickly untying her ankles. Why hadn't he attacked her? She frantically stabbed at the interior with a dart in each fist, the points ripping through it, leaving slits big enough to get her fingers through. She tore the bag from her and turned.

Bloom was six feet away from her, but he still looked dazed. He frowned as he staggered towards Rose, as if struggling to remember the situation.

Rose looked up the stairs. The door at the top was open and she rapidly started to climb. *Please follow me away from*

Noah. Two thirds of the way up, she heard Bloom's heavy footfalls behind her.

She rocketed through the door and into the lounge. Should she lead him outside? From the noises behind her, however, Rose was positive she wouldn't have time to open the front door. He probably still had the knife on him. *Go to the kitchen. Grab another weapon.* But had he emptied all the drawers? She made a beeline for the room but as she headed down the pathway between the stacked boxes, he slammed into her from the side.

Rose struck the stack to her right and it toppled. She went with it and Bloom's weight was on top of her. She struggled out from under him and was on her feet.

So was Bloom. He rounded on her, blocking her route to the kitchen. His expression still seemed disoriented. Had the blows to the head concussed him?

'Rose.' He held out his left palm. The bread knife was in his right. 'Rose, this is futile.'

She rushed at him, grabbed the blade with both hands and gripped it so he couldn't thrust it forward.

Confusion briefly registered but Bloom deftly slid the knife out and she cried as it cut into her hands. She grabbed hold of it again, blood streaming from her fists.

He used his free hand to clumsily take a swipe at her, but she crouched low and pushed back hard on the blade.

Bloom stumbled back into the stack of boxes on the left. For a moment he teetered and then he went down as the whole column collapsed. The contents of some of the boxes spilled out. He was still holding the knife. As he struggled to get upright again, Rose registered that a lot of the garden tools she'd packed were now across the floor.

She saw the pair of shears at the same time he did, and he kicked them away with his right foot as he stood up. Her eyes pinged about the other implements, and she spotted the sledgehammer protruding from under the flap of one of the opened boxes. Rose went for it and hefted the heavy head as Bloom came at her with the knife.

The sledgehammer came down on his wrist and he howled and staggered back, still brandishing the knife.

Rose heaved the hammer above her.

'Come on, Rose…' His eyes were on the head as it wavered.

She could barely keep it raised but knew that if she missed, he could easily finish her before she could lift it again.

'Take your shot.'

Rose did before he could prepare himself. The head slammed hard into the top of his left shoulder, and she felt the bone break as the sledgehammer embedded itself there.

Bloom opened his mouth and then dropped to his knees, his expression distorted by pain.

Rose yanked the tool clear and swung it high to bring it down on his skull. But its weight tipped back, and it landed with a thud behind her.

Bloom lunged forward with the blade.

Rose leapt back and dodged it, but her bare foot skated on a slice of pizza. Her ankle twisted and she went down.

Bloom cried as he tried to crawl towards her, using his injured shoulder.

She kicked back at him but felt the point of the knife enter the heel of her left foot. She pushed herself backwards on her palms as he came at her again. Her body butted hard against another stack of boxes, and they collapsed on top of Bloom. He shook them off and kept coming. Rose was cornered with her shoulders against the bottom box.

Bloom had the knife raised, so she grabbed one of the smaller boxes and tried to use it as a shield.

Bloom stabbed the box and jerked it away.

She seized another but he did the same.

Now she had nothing left to defend herself with but her fists. 'Get the fuck away from me!' Her knuckle connected with the point of the knife as he slithered forward and stabbed at her.

'Just hold still, Rose.'

She could smell his acrid breath, see the dried blood caked around his flaring nostrils.

'It's been a hell of a night.'

Chapter Seventy-Three

Rose pushed herself back with her bare heels and felt the box behind her slide a few inches. She pushed harder with the base of her spine and it moved a foot. With the boxes on top of it gone, she could shift it and retreat.

Bloom grunted in agony as he crawled towards her, blood bubbling at his nose. He raised the knife.

She jerked her leg back and the blade pierced the wooden tile where it had just been. Rose kicked back, caught him square in the face with the sole of her foot and felt his nose crush and pop beneath it.

Bloom opened his mouth to react, but she stamped at him again and he turned his head right to protect himself as she used both feet. He gasped but kept his face buried in his good shoulder to avoid the assault. He raised the arm holding the knife and attempted to stab her legs again.

Rose kicked at the hand with the blade, slid her butt forward and pedalled at his broken shoulder.

Bloom yelled and slumped onto his face.

She snatched the opportunity to stand, her calf in agony as she pushed herself up.

Bloom grabbed her ankle with his free hand, his fingers squeezing hard to restrain her.

She put her free foot on the back of his other hand, pinning the knife to the floor. She knew she wasn't heavy enough to hold him there so she bent her legs, put her knee against his injured shoulder and pressed as hard as she could.

Bloom emitted a full-throated scream this time.

Rose leaned into him, but she could feel him tugging his knife hand from under her foot.

As he pulled it free, she twisted around onto his back, her knees either side of his spine. She pulled Noah's dressing gown belt from her pocket and hooked it around his throat.

Bloom tried to rise so she pulled on the nylon garrotte as hard as she could and jabbed her left elbow into his wounded shoulder. She was still rising, however. He got to his feet.

She tipped herself forward, using her weight to keep the top half of his torso down, but knew he could throw her as he had in the cellar. She tightened the belt and heard the material squeaking as it cut into his larynx.

Bloom gasped and thrust his knife hand back.

Rose felt the blade point go into the soft tissue under her kneecap but kept her body rigid as she held onto him and ground her elbow into his shoulder again.

He staggered sideways then back again. He was losing his balance.

Don't let go.

Bloom lurched forward and struck another stack of boxes hard.

Rose's head slammed into it as hard as he did, and they both went down as the column collapsed on top of them. Something heavy struck her back and she was winded as she was flattened on top of him.

Darkness.

She could hear him breathing close and heavy, feel the heat of it on her face.

Bloom tried to shift from underneath her.

She still held the belt taut in her fists. She tightened it again, but he was pushing them out of the pile. Suddenly she was spun over, and he landed on top of her. The back of his head was against her face, and she tried to keep hold of the belt, but he got his hands underneath it and tore it from her grip. His scalp unstuck from her face. He was getting up and she was positive he still had the knife.

Rose pushed herself away from the boxes and felt sharp points in her back. Whatever she was reversing through had been broken. But as she emerged from the pile, she could see what she was lying in. It was the fragments of Lucas's broken pottery that she'd been unable to throw away. They were scattered all around the floor.

Without hesitation, Rose grabbed the largest fragment and crawled on her hands and knees to where Bloom was sitting up with his back to her. He was just leaning on one side, starting to rise.

In that moment, it was his words that were foremost in her mind. The ones he'd used when she'd first encountered him in the cellar.

'When it's the shot that really matters, you just say to yourself, this one's for my life.'

Rose jabbed the jagged fragment into his neck, and he froze. When she pulled it out, the blood immediately gushed from the wound. He tried to cover it with his palm, but Rose stabbed him again, first in his fingers, then in the back of his neck, then on the other side of his throat and the top of his head.

Even after Bloom had slumped forward, Rose kept stabbing at him. She didn't stop until he'd rolled onto his side and was motionless.

When she eventually stood, Rose couldn't release the fragment. It was lodged in her palm, stuck to her hand with his blood and hers.

Only the sound of her laboured breathing filled the room. She ignored the pain as she went through his trouser pockets. If he moved, she'd use the fragment again.

His head lolled as she searched. Bloom was quite dead

and when she found her mobile, she stepped over him and limped to the open cellar door.

She nearly buckled when she was halfway down the stairs. Rose could hear her son breathing though. As she hit the bottom of the steps, she could see that Noah had crawled clear of the bag and was lying on his side.

His eyes met hers and he moaned his relief through the gag.

Rose ran to him and pulled the gag from his mouth, releasing all the incoherent terror and anguish that had been pent up within him from the first moment he'd been taken from her. She hugged him hard, felt his heart throbbing through his whole body. Even as she untied his hands, she didn't let him go.

Epilogue

Two and a half months later

'Hi, Mrs Dunbar, it's just me.'

Rose was looking at DI Forbes through the peephole of the apartment door. 'Just a minute.' She released the three locks.

The female police officer's expression was patient as the door opened. 'Sorry it's an evening call.'

Rose stood back. 'Come through.' It was late. She liked to have the place locked down by six in the evening. After she made sure the DI closed the door behind her, she led the officer down the passage to the kitchen.

'How's the physio?'

'Slow but sure.' Rose was still hobbling but had been assured that the injuries to her legs weren't permanent. It often felt like she still had a metal blade in her kneecap though.

Noah was sitting at the kitchen table.

'Not a fan of anchovies, Noah?' the DI observed.

He'd pulled most of them off the pizza and had piled them up on the opened lid of the delivery box.

'Honest to God, we never asked for them.'

The two women smiled at his reply.

Rose didn't want to scold him for using the phrase as she'd done in the past. Sooner or later, the junk food had to stop though. But for the foreseeable future, she was prepared to let Noah have whatever he wanted at mealtimes. After what he'd been through, Rose couldn't bring herself to nag him about his diet. He'd cottoned onto that and was using it to get his way, but she was just relieved he was acting the way any child should.

For several weeks after the event, she'd worried he'd completely withdrawn into himself. Slowly, however, and with coaxing from her and his therapist, the old Noah had come back. She never wanted to hear anyone tell her again that children were resilient. She worried that his trauma was more entrenched than anyone was aware of, but for the moment it was progress and he'd already made a partial return to school. She'd considered withholding the truth about his grandmother but, after concealing the circumstances of his father's seizure, Rose had decided to tell him that Bloom had been responsible for her death. He didn't need to know the specifics yet. She was still grappling with those herself and knew that, sometime in the future, they would both begin to grieve properly for her. She'd told him that they had to heal first though and that it was going to be a very gradual process.

'I've found another one.' Noah grimaced as he fished out the morsel.

'Why don't you take it into the lounge?' Rose suggested to him.

His eyes lit up at the prospect of another Xbox dinner. Usually, Rose insisted on them eating together at the table, so this was another rule he was happy to bypass for as long as he could. Noah took four of the eight slices of pizza, piled them onto his plate and scuttled off to the other room.

'You hungry?' Rose gestured at the pizza.

'No, thanks.' DI Forbes shook her head. 'I don't want to hold up your dinner.'

Rose nodded for her to sit at the breakfast bar and the police officer pulled out a chair. She did too.

'Things a little more normal now?' DI Forbes was looking at the doorway Noah had just left through.

'We're getting there. So...' she prompted as the officer gave her a straight-lipped smile.

'Just wanted to give you an update. I promised we'd keep you informed.'

Rose swallowed, waiting for her to continue.

'Haden Bloom was cremated yesterday.'

Rose nodded and felt a surge of relief. Why should she feel that? He was dead. Maybe the notion of burning away the injuries she'd inflicted on him gave her a sense of release. She'd become a different person that night. She'd done everything to protect Noah. She would never regret that. But she'd stabbed him twenty-two times. That was something that deeply unsettled her. She remembered little of killing him and felt anxious that one day it might all come back to her.

'It was his father's wish.'

It seemed bizarre that a cold predator like Bloom could actually have a father.

'He was the only family member present.'

Rose nodded. 'Thanks for letting me know.'

'There's been another development...' DI Forbes kept her eyes on the table. 'One we thought you should be aware of.'

Rose felt a fresh surge of dread. It happened several times a day, but she was trying to reduce the medication she'd been taking to dull the panic attacks.

'Amongst his belongings we found the key to a "Zone 1" storage unit.'

Rose had heard of them. They were a national company that let space in urban warehouses.

'We managed to get inside.'

'What did you find?' Rose prompted unnecessarily.

'Nothing. The space was empty.'

Rose exhaled. 'So... you think that's where he was going to take the cases?'

'Seems plausible.' DI Forbes nodded but still seemed troubled.

Rose tried not to think about her and Noah inside their bags, stored away with Bloom's other victims. 'So, what's the problem?'

'The size of it.'

Rose frowned but knew what the DI was insinuating.

'It was such a large area and he'd installed three storage racks. Each about thirty feet long.'

Rose swallowed.

'Why rent such a big space for four... or even six ...' the DI looked uncomfortable '... cases? We just wonder, given his day job, how many houses he might have kept keys for.'

Rose felt her skin tighten and the wound on the back of her calf tingle.

'Having the sort of access a removal man does, it stands to reason that your home may not have been the only one he used.' The DI let her absorb the implications of that. 'So, we're requesting details from Maynard's of all the properties he's ever entered.'

Rose imagined the vacant space that Bloom rented. Were there more cases he'd hidden elsewhere?

'Rose, are you all right?'

She thought of the people who lived in the properties he'd been inside. Couples and families all going about their daily lives as she had, completely oblivious to what might lay beneath them.

After DI Forbes had left, promising to pass on any further news, Rose secured the locks on the door and leaned her back against the panel. She wanted a drink, but she deliberately didn't have any in the house now – hadn't allowed herself since they'd left the hospital. She'd been medicated enough. Rose never wanted to go back to the house. Even though forensics had established that no other bodies were present, it would be in limbo until the investigation was over and she'd withdrawn from the sale so Spear Cosmetics couldn't get the land. It looked like she would be renting for the foreseeable future. But even though Bloom had done all he could to destroy her family, they were still alive, and he was gone. She'd used the broken fragments of the past to kill him and now he was ash.

Had Bloom simply needed to share his crimes with her as he had with his best friend before he'd killed him? The notion that his choice to murder was so arbitrary, that he'd so casually taken others' lives, was something that would always chill her to the core. His psychosis hadn't arisen from some personal trauma or abuse but, more obscenely, from a violent moment of idle curiosity. It was the closest she'd ever got to pure evil, and she was determined that it would never get near her or her son again.

She walked back to the lounge and leaned in. Noah didn't look up from his Xbox. Rose knew how frustrated he'd get if she tried to give him a hug during a game. She resisted the temptation and told herself she'd snatch one when she ordered him to bed. No more leniency on that front. Now that he was returning to school, it was back to a stricter regime. Next week, anyway.

Rose opened the door beside the lounge and padded in.

Lucas was lying in the bed with his eyes half open. She sat gently on the single bed and tried to find a sign of the man she used to know in his gaze. His condition had worsened, and the advice had been not to bring him home. But despite the challenges that presented, Rose wanted him with them. It had made Noah happy and that made her happy. Home had to be the best place for Lucas, even though it wasn't the home he'd left. She hadn't told him what had happened to them and had asked Noah not to either. Not just yet. There were to be no more secrets, but they all had to help each other mend now.

'OK. Nearly time to sleep.' She could hear the fatigue in her voice.

Rose slid her fingers into his palm and gently squeezed his thumb.

A few moments later she searched his eyes again. Had it been her imagination or had he just gently squeezed back?

Acknowledgments

A huge thanks to you for choosing this book. I hope you stayed up late to finish it and aren't too afraid to turn out the light.

A debt of gratitude, as always, to the positive energy that is my wife, Anne-Marie, who is still a little afraid of reading my stories. Also to my loyal readers Mum and Dad, who always devour my latest outing and have now built up a library of these books in their lounge.

And now to the creative squad at One More Chapter – Bethan Morgan, my adroit and efficient editor, who gave me some invaluable notes after reading the first draft and who is always so easy to work with; my copyeditor Laura Burge and proofreader Tony Russell; Charlotte Ledger, Publishing Director, for continuing to have faith in my work; and the talented Lucy Bennett for another arresting cover design.

Must also acknowledge my old editor and new agent, Hannah Todd at Madeleine Milburn.

And, as ever, I can't underestimate how grateful I am for the time spent by reviewers and bloggers who are key to every author's career and convey their passion for books by shouting about the ones they love for no wage. Thanks for your generosity online and elsewhere. A special salute to Karen Cole, Jen Lucas, Nicki Richards, Claire Knight, Sarah Hardy, Eleni (lafemmereaders620), Liz Barnsley, Melissa Suslowicz Bartz, Donna Maguire, Zoe-lee O'Farrell, Nigel Adams, Suze-Clarke-Morris, Kaisha Jayneh, Amanda Oughton, The Book Cosy, Louise Mullins, Carole Whiteley, Rachel Broughton, Alison Drew, Magdalena Johansson, Diane Hogg, Martha Cheeves, Joyce Juzwik, Amy Sullivan, Kelly Lacey, Rebecca Pugh, Chelsea Humphrey, Ellie Smith, Steve Robb, Emma Welton, Stephanie Rothwell, Cleo Bannister, Abby Fairbrother, Sheila Howes, Linda Strong, Maxine Groves, Joanne Robertson, Susan Hampson, Malina Skrobosinski, James Atkins, Shell Baker, Fran Hagan, Mandie Griffiths, Jo Ford, Marilina Tzelepi and Scott Griffin. Special thanks also to fellow author and crime writing authority, Noelle Holten, for her continued support.

Please swing by my website for all the latest: richard@richardjayparker.com or find me on Instagram (@bemykiller), Twitter (@Bookwalter) and Facebook (@RJParkerUK).

ALL YOUR FRIENDS
ARE INVITED.

BUT WHICH OF THEM
WILL SURVIVE?

THE
DINNER
PARTY

R. J. PARKER

Don't miss *The Dinner Party*, another addictive and twisty psychological thriller by R. J. Parker...

Eight friends. Eight secrets. One killer.

A group of old friends gather in a peaceful suburban street for a dinner party. They are expecting a fun evening of wine, food and pleasant company. But then they start to play the game...

It's about trust and dark secrets – it tests marriage to its limits – and none of them can begin to imagine its consequences. Because the next day, two guests are dead and the others are trapped in a nightmare...

HE WATCHED
HE WAITED
HE MADE HIS MOVE

WHILE
YOU
SLEPT

R. J. PARKER

You will also love *While You Slept* – what would you do if you woke up in your home but it wasn't your home at all?

When a man wearing a picture mask of her daughter Maisie's face stands tauntingly in her garden, Lily Russell does the smart thing and calls the police. When she and Maisie wake up the following morning in an exact replica of their home, held captive by that same man, the police are no longer an option.

Surrounded by the rooms and things that once provided comfort and now only promote fear, Lily and Maisie must fight to survive. Because when no one knows where you are, you are your only hope.

R. J. PARKER

THE
GOOD
NEIGHBOUR

YOU KNOCKED ON THE DOOR,
A KILLER ANSWERED...

The Good Neighbour **is a similarly nerve-shredding**
suspense thriller of secrets and serial killers...

When Leah Talbot crashes her car one night, she spots a
light on in a nearby house and approaches, hoping that
someone is home.

He is.

But when she returns the next morning to thank the man
who helped her, the police answer the door.

There's been a brutal murder and the female homeowner is
lying dead in a pool of blood upstairs...

ONE MORE CHAPTER

YOUR NUMBER ONE STOP

FOR PAGETURNING BOOKS

The author and One More Chapter would like to thank everyone who contributed to the publication of this story...

Analytics
Emma Harvey
Connor Hayes
Maria Osa

Audio
Charlotte Brown

Contracts
Olivia Bignold-Jordan
Florence Shepherd

Design
Lucy Bennett
Fiona Greenway
Holly Macdonald
Liane Payne
Dean Russell
Caroline Young

Digital Sales
Hannah Lismore
Fliss Porter
Georgina Ugen
Kelly Webster

Editorial
Laura Burge
Charlotte Ledger
Bethan Morgan
Jennie Rothwell
Tony Russell
Kimberley Young

Harper360
Emily Gerbner
Jean Marie Kelly
Juliette Pasquini
emma sullivan

HarperCollins Canada
Peter Borcsok

International Sales
Hannah Avery
Alice Gomer
Phillipa Walker

Marketing & Publicity
Emma Petfield
Sara Roberts
Helena Towers

Operations
Melissa Okusanya
Hannah Stamp

Production
Denis Manson
Simon Moore
Sophie Waeland

Rights
Lana Beckwith
Samuel Birkett
Agnes Rigou
Zoe Shine
Aisling Smyth

The HarperCollins Distribution Team

The HarperCollins Finance & Royalties Team

The HarperCollins Legal Team

The HarperCollins Technology Team

Trade Marketing
Ben Hurd

UK Sales
Yazmeen Akhtar
Laura Carpenter
Isabel Coburn
Jay Cochrane
Sarah Munro
Gemma Rayner
Erin White
Leah Woods

And every other essential link in the chain from delivery drivers to booksellers to librarians and beyond!

ONE MORE CHAPTER

One More Chapter is an
award-winning global
division of HarperCollins.

Subscribe to our newsletter to get our
latest eBook deals and stay up to date
with all our new releases!

signup.harpercollins.co.uk/
join/signup-omc

Meet the team at
www.onemorechapter.com

Follow us!

 @OneMoreChapter_
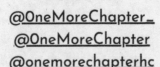 @OneMoreChapter
@onemorechapterhc

Do you write unputdownable fiction?
We love to hear from new voices.
Find out how to submit your novel at
www.onemorechapter.com/submissions